5

Sweet Regrets

Indigo Bay Sweet Romance Series

JENNIFER PEEL

Chapter One

"MEL, MEL." HEATHER NUDGED ME.

"What?" I was focused on my sandwich.

"Look. Is that who I think it is?"

Both Halle and I faced the direction Heather was fixed on, the doors of Sweet Caroline's Cafe.

I dropped my chicken salad sandwich. A million memories flooded my mind, each one featuring the man waiting to be seated. Declan Shaw. I hadn't seen him since we left for college almost twelve years ago. Our goodbye wasn't what I hoped it would be. I looked at my empty ring finger. It had been recently vacated, but a long time ago, the handsome man in khakis and a polo shirt—who looked to have filled out quite nicely—had placed a promise ring there. I still remember staring at the tiny diamond on a white gold band. I was so torn. I loved Declan Shaw, but we were too young and I didn't know what would happen when I went off to Clemson and he left the state to go to Virginia Tech. How could we possibly promise each other forever when we were eighteen?

He couldn't see why we wouldn't. I broke his heart that night and he in turn broke mine when I never heard from him again.

"Did you know he was in town?" Halle asked me.

I shook my head no, still mesmerized by the grown-up version of the cute boy from next door. His sandy brown hair was shorter than it used to be, and his chest had broadened. But I was sure he still had the same deep blue eyes with full, long eyelashes that always did me in. He was tall and lean, but even from a distance I could see he was more defined. But how would I know he was in town? I was barely back in Indigo Bay myself. And I was still reeling from my divorce and…I had other things on my mind. I placed a hand on my midsection and breathed.

My best friends in the world both looked at me with interest. Halle and Heather Orton, twins extraordinaire, fabulous interior designers, and recent owners of their own interior design firm, H2O Designs. I loved that name. But most importantly they had been a rock and life line, especially the last several months. Two sets of identical brown eyes focused on me.

Halle—the artist, as we liked to call her, with the short dark hair that was currently streaked blue—leaned across the table. "You should go say hi."

"No way," Heather argued. She was the assertive one, with what you might call classic beauty. They were both gorgeous, but Heather always wore her hair in long waves like a Pantene commercial and she dressed like Macy's was her closet. "If he wants to talk to her, he'll have to come here."

I agreed with Heather, except I was taking it a step further. "Let's slip out." Out of all the people I'd want to face under my current circumstances, he would be close to last on the list. But it was too late.

On the way to his table, Declan looked our direction and it was as if our eyes magnetically locked. It caused mass

2

flutters in my stomach, and not the kind I had been having as of late. I wasn't sure that kind existed for me anymore. His smile only created more. When he headed our way, I felt as if my stomach would burst with butterflies.

Heather was closest to me and grabbed my hand under the table.

What was I going to do now? I sat up straight and pulled down on my peach tank top. I wondered how unruly my curly auburn locks were. I blew out a breath, making my long bangs take flight. We were all fixed on the beyond handsome man walking our way.

I held my stomach and felt some other kinds of flutters, my favorite kind. I wanted to ask if I looked okay, but what did it really matter? He approached and we lost eye contact.

He looked to Heather and Halle first. "Halle, Heather. It's been a long time."

Both ladies looked to me before they faced Declan.

"It has been; it's nice to see you again." Halle was cordial.

Heather was a tad curt. "What are you doing back here?"

Declan focused on me. "I took a position in Charleston." Charleston was about thirty minutes away.

I held my breath. I wasn't sure how I felt about him being so close.

"How are you, Mel?" Nerves and sentimentalism ran through his words.

For a moment, I lost the ability to speak. All I could do was stare at my first love. I never thought I would see him again, and certainly not under the circumstances. But it was a long time ago and it didn't matter that he was back. He was probably married now with a kid or two.

Heather squeezed my hand, telling me to speak.

"I'm great." That was a lie, but I'd been telling it to everyone.

"I'm happy to hear that. Do you live here or are you visiting?"

"Living here for now." I wasn't sure where I would permanently land once I regrouped.

He tilted his head. "That's great." His cheeks tinged pink.

A familiar voice called his name from across the cafe.

We all turned and faced Rich Dixon, best father around. Why did he call Declan's name and not mine? It was almost as if he was there to…

"Declan." Daddy patted him on the back. "Thanks for meeting me on a Saturday here instead of the office." Daddy's construction company was located in Charleston as well.

"Daddy?" I was more than confused why they were meeting and why Daddy didn't tell me.

"Darlin'." He smiled at me. His hazel eyes were just like mine, but his were full of mischief. It made him look much younger than his silver hair said he was. "Declan's the new district manager for Redline. And he's trying to convince me why Redline is a better fit." The excitement in his voice spoke of how much he loved talking business with anyone.

I knew enough about Daddy's business to know that Redline was a heavy equipment vendor. And that Dixon Construction would be a huge account for them. That also meant that Declan did well for himself. District manager was an enviable position in that industry.

Declan gave me a smile before facing Daddy. "I won't have to do any convincing, the numbers and our customer satisfaction will speak for themselves." Oh, he was a good salesman. I could tell.

"Well, let's get to talking." Daddy tipped his head. "Ladies, have a good lunch." For me he had a wink.

Declan gave me one more smile. "It was good to see you, Mel."

All I did was stare at him, still in shock.

"Halle and Heather, nice to see you as well."

My best friends and I nodded in sync as we watched him walk away to meet with Daddy. I finally let out a huge breath. Our Saturday afternoon lunch had taken a very interesting turn. All of our heads came together so we could talk in hushed tones.

"Let's just say, he's fine, like super fine." Heather was first to speak. "But let's not forget Mel cried her entire freshman year over him."

It wasn't all year long, but there were lots of sob-filled phone calls to my best friends those first few months after we broke up, or more like disintegrated.

"We can't hold what he did when he was eighteen against him now." Halle always tried to see the good in everyone.

"It doesn't matter. It was a long time ago and I'm sure he's married by now or at the very least has a girlfriend. And, well," I looked down at my abdomen, "I'm taken." My little one kicked, always reminding where my priorities were.

"I didn't see a ring." Heather was always looking for those.

"Regardless, we're ancient history."

Halle took a peek at him. "It looks like your dad is telling him something about you and they are both looking our way."

Of course he was. "Better for him to find out from my dad than Miss Lucille." Lucille Sanderson was the biggest busybody in Indigo Bay. "She's been telling as many people as she can that Greyson left me because the baby wasn't his."

"You mean the sperm donor?" Heather had the deepest look of loathing going on. That's what we had relegated my ex-husband to. He was barely deserving of that title.

"Miss Lucille has nothing better to do with her time, and no one listens to her." Halle tried to be of some comfort.

"It still doesn't stop people from staring at me and talking about me whenever I'm around. It's like I'm the first person ever to get divorced or have a baby."

Halle reached across the table and took my hand. "Everyone's just concerned. We all love you."

"Halle, you are so naïve sometimes." Heather rolled her eyes.

"So everyone doesn't love me?" I smiled.

We all laughed. That felt good. I missed laughter.

When the laughter faded, Heather pulled our heads together again. "Don't you think it's awfully coincidental that you and Declan both moved back here at the same time? Maybe the world is trying to give you a message."

My best friends looked at me to respond.

I shrugged. "I'm pretty sure that message is to stay away from men." I rubbed my little one. "Even Declan left me." I thought back to the summer before our junior year when his family moved in. From the moment I saw him, I was smitten. Right away we clicked. I even broke up with my boyfriend, Dallas Harper. His momma owned this very cafe. And now he owned the beachside cottage resort. Dallas wasn't broken up about it. He was already off at school and he made sure to mention he hadn't planned on staying true to me while we were apart. Too bad my ex-husband didn't give me that disclaimer before we got married. Anyway. Declan and I were like peanut butter and chocolate—made for each other. Each tasted better with the other. But we were so young. I didn't want either one of us to feel obligated once we headed for higher education. But I thought if we were truly meant to be it would work out. We would make it back to each other.

He obviously didn't agree.

"It's weird he came back here. His parents haven't lived here for ages," Halle commented.

"The job market's good in Charleston," I reasoned. "And if he's the district manager, it probably means this was a promotion for him and the only location available at the time."

"Maybe." Halle sat back and took a sip of her sweet tea.

I missed that stuff, but my doctor recommended no caffeine while I was pregnant. I shrugged my shoulders. "All I know is it has nothing to do with me. Let's change the subject."

They both knew to drop it. But they glanced over at the table where Declan sat. I couldn't help but look too. He gave me a smile. I turned from him. The last thing I needed was a charming smile from another man who left me.

"You can both make it Monday to my ultrasound, right?" My momma had a huge phobia of anything medical related, so the best friends a girl could ask for were stepping in. I was having it done a month later than I normally should have, but my life had been a chaotic mess until I moved home last month. But I was getting back on track.

They both lit up.

"Yes. We cleared our schedule." Halle grinned.

"You ladies are the best."

"We know." Heather checked her reflection in her phone. She was as gorgeous as ever. "You said your doctor was handsome, right?"

A little too handsome for my taste, at least when it came to doctors. He came highly recommended and I was lucky to get in to him. But I felt like I was in an episode of Grey's Anatomy. Dr. Winters—aka Dr. Dreamy—was a far cry different than sweet old Dr. Ryland who had been my doctor in Philadelphia before my life crashed down around me. I preferred the grandpa knowing me more intimately than anyone really needed to over the model. But I guess I already suffered the ultimate humiliation when my husband showed up to our divorce proceedings with his mistress, so I could survive the beautiful doctor getting up close and personal.

"He's more than handsome."

"What should I wear?" Heather asked us.

Halle and I both rolled our eyes and turned back to our food.

Though my appetite was kind of shot now. I couldn't help but glance over several times at Declan. I always wondered what became of him. Did he get his MBA like he planned? Did he run a marathon? We both ran cross country in high school and a marathon was a goal of his. He was certainly still in shape. Like I said, it didn't matter. All that mattered now was the little one that called my insides home.

Chapter Two

"DECLAN COULDN'T KEEP HIS EYES OFF YOU." HALLE STRUNG her arm through mine.

The three of us were headed toward the spring festival held at Waterfront Park every year. I hadn't been in forever. But it was the perfect day for it. Sunny, warm, hardly a cloud in the sky. Children's laughter rang through the air. I couldn't believe one day one of those little voices would belong to me.

"It means nothing. I'm sure he was just surprised like everyone else that I'm living back with my parents, divorced, and pregnant." No one was more surprised than me. I had done my best not to look at him when we left, even though I wanted to. During college I thought of him so many times. I had fantasies of him coming to find me to tell me how sorry he was so we could pick up where we left off. But he never came. So I headed north to Philadelphia when a large financial planning firm recruited me straight out of college. It was there I met the biggest mistake of my life at a financial institution conference. I rubbed my abdomen. At least I got the best parting gift ever.

"Or maybe, like every other single man in this town, he's still in love with you," Heather commented.

"We don't know he's single. And no one is in love with me."

"Please. All you have to do is say the word and you would have ten guys lined up to date you." Heather wasn't letting it drop.

"I'm pregnant."

Halle scooted in closer to me. "And gorgeous inside and out."

"You girls really are the best, but it's apparent I have horrible taste in men, so it's best not to think about any of them."

"Did you look at him though?" Heather fanned herself with her hand. "If it didn't go against the girlfriend code, I would make a play for him."

"Be my guest."

Heather took my other arm. "You don't mean that. I know you, and despite what you're saying, we all know how in love with him you were. And I saw in your eyes that you still have a little spark for him, whether you admit it or not."

"You caught my eye when the baby was moving." The baby was my truest love of all time.

"You're such a liar, but I understand." Heather laughed.

I looked out at all the brightly colored booths. The last time I had been to the festival I felt like I had my whole life ahead of me. And I thought Declan would be a part of it. Those were unrealistic teenage machinations.

"Where do you want to head first?" Halle asked.

"Ooo, let's hit Faye's jewelry booth. She promised me she would make me some of those lace chokers." Heather and her jewelry.

We headed in that direction amongst the crowd while I reveled in the warmth and sea air—all things I missed living in Philadelphia. While Halle and Heather bought out Faye's jewelry booth, I headed to Jimmy's booth. He believed the 1960s were the best years of his life and so he dressed accordingly and only listened to music from that era. Which meant he was a pro at finding what I considered retro albums from artists like the Beatles and Simon and Garfunkel. But don't get him going on the latter group. He was still torn up that they refused to make up and tour again. To him their voices were national treasures.

And sure enough, I could hear "The Sound of Silence" as I approached. I had missed home and all the people who made my childhood so magical. It was no wonder this was where I ran to.

There sat Jimmy with his long, braided gray hair wearing a psychedelic tie-dyed t-shirt. His booth was covered in colored beads and he had boxes full of old records.

"Hi, Jimmy." I never knew his last name. I'm not sure anyone did.

"Miss Melanie. I heard you were back in town. Looks like you packed some extra luggage." He pointed to my belly. "Congratulations."

"Thank you. Got anything good?" I peered into one of his cardboard boxes that had seen better days.

"I have just the thing for you." He rummaged through the box closest to him. He soon pulled out a tattered cover and handed it to me. "The Mamas and Papas. There are some great songs on that album that would make the perfect lullabies. Or you can't go wrong with Simon and Garfunkel." He looked up to the sky as if he was paying homage to the duo.

I looked over the worn cover. I had bought a retro looking record player, more for decoration than anything, but it might be nice to have something to play on it. "I'll take it.

And if you have anything by Simon and Garfunkel, I'll take that too."

It looked like he was going to tear up. "You are a gem, Miss Melanie."

I did miss this place.

With my new treasures, I headed back to find my best friends. I was feeling more alive than I had in months. I needed this place and these people, even if I was the hot topic of Indigo Bay gossip. And I had a feeling there was only going to be more of it. Declan was walking my way. For a second I felt seventeen again. His smile and eyes always did me in and when he looked at me, I always knew they were only for me. I had convinced myself his smile was different for me than for anyone else. He was wearing it now, but that was silly. We were silly.

I bit my lip. "Declan, what are you doing here?" I looked around, praying no one was paying attention. His family moved away a few months after he graduated from high school. I hoped that meant most people wouldn't recognize him or his connection to me.

He glanced down at my baby bump.

"Yes, I'm pregnant."

His eyes headed north. "I didn't mean to stare. Congratulations."

"Thank you." I walked past him.

He followed. "Do you think we could talk?"

"About what?"

He laughed. "You sound like a tough sell, like your dad."

"You didn't answer the question."

He studied me carefully. I could see the salesman gears turning through those gorgeous eyes of his. "I thought maybe we could catch up."

I wasn't buying it. "Declan, considering the last time we were together and all the time that has passed, I don't know what we have to catch up on."

"I know. That's what I wanted to talk to you about."

"Why? It was long time ago."

"Maybe I was wrong—you're tougher than your dad."

I stopped and looked up at him. Even though I was five-foot-eight, he was several inches taller than me. "No. I just can't look back anymore. I wish you the best."

"Please, Mel."

His charm almost had me, but I had fallen victim to the allure of a handsome man one too many times. "Bye, Declan."

∽◌∾

I was soaking up the sun by our pool waiting for my parents to get home. Momma and her friends had been running a booth selling crafts to benefit the local animal shelter. She was always busy doing good. It's one of the things I loved about her. And Daddy was playing a round of golf after his meeting with Declan. I still couldn't believe he hadn't told me who he was meeting with. Maybe he figured so much time had passed it didn't matter, but you would have at least thought he would mention it as a point of interest.

I tried not to think about Declan as I scrolled through a Realtor site on my tablet. I needed to find my own place, even though Momma was begging me to stay. I think Daddy and she were looking forward to being grandparents as much as I was looking forward to being a mom. It was still hard to believe. I was happy to finally be surrounded by people that were excited about the impending arrival.

I looked out toward the ocean and watched the waves roll in. I thought back to the night I told Greyson I was pregnant. I was so excited, even though I knew he wanted to hold off until we had been married five years and we were shy by a couple. I knew in an instant that not only was he not happy about it, but he was angry. He blamed me for not being careful. He immediately left, said he needed to think. It didn't take him long to decide we were done.

It was then I found out about the affair he was having with one of the tellers at the bank he was president of. She worked in one of the branches. I'm not sure how they met, but he refused to admit paternity. And suddenly I found myself very alone. His mom, Tamara, whom I had been close to, pulled away and believed her son's lies that it was me that had been unfaithful. Our married friends seemed to vanish. And I was left with a choice. Force the paternity issue or let him buy me off. At first I was determined to make him admit he was the father—because he absolutely was—but then I realized after all his ugly actions, he was the last man I ever wanted to be the father of my child.

With my support group gone and the major humiliation he had put me through, I packed up and left after the divorce was final. I basically took his bribe and a whole lot of his money. I wasn't sure what kind of person that made me, but it gave me time to think about what my next steps were. And it set my baby and me up for a long time. One thing I knew for sure was that my plans would never involve my ex-husband. I beat myself up on a frequent basis about how blind I had been. There were probably a hundred warning signs along the way and I missed them or chose not to pay attention because I loved him.

He had this charisma to him. He was a rock star in the financial world. Not only was he the president of one of the largest banks in Pennsylvania, but he was constantly asked to speak at conferences. He was innovative and knew how to motivate people. And when he set his sights on me, I was flattered and taken in by him. He was a lot older than me, eleven years to be exact, and that also excited me. But after we married he worked more than he was ever home. I was low on his priority list. In the end, I was only there to give him the image he wanted. I was educated and came from a good family. I was just part of his resume. When he found out I was pregnant, he didn't have time to add fatherhood to the list. He barely had time to be a husband and a philanderer.

He was one more man to forget about. I was seriously considering telling this baby of mine that I had been artificially inseminated. How could I ever explain to my child that he didn't want him or her? I wasn't looking forward to the questions I knew would come.

For just a second I wondered what would have happened if I had taken Declan's ring and waited for him. But I couldn't go down that road. I couldn't look back, like I told Declan. My life was already trailed with too many regrets. No sense in adding one more. And who's to say that it would have worked out anyway?

Chapter Three

"I CAN'T BELIEVE YOU INVITED HIM TO LUNCH." I PEELED the carrot I held with a vengeance over the kitchen sink.

Daddy laughed and Momma kept stirring the lemon sauce for her blueberry Bundt cake.

Daddy kissed my cheek. "Don't get yourself worked up. I don't need you upsetting my grandson."

"We don't know it's a boy." I was certain it was a girl, because a girl would look like me and not the sperm donor.

"I'd bet money. We need someone to carry on the Dixon name."

"You're trying to change the subject."

"Honey, he was our neighbor." Momma was always first to back up her husband.

"So? That was a long time ago."

She turned from the stove and smiled at me. "So were some other things." She was beautiful and right, but still. She brushed back her red hair like she was still flirting with Daddy.

He took the cue and kissed her.

Why couldn't I have love like that? I went back to peeling the carrots for the salad. "Maybe I should go into town.

I could go look at the red bungalow near the pier." I knew I probably shouldn't. It was a lot more than I wanted to pay, but the pictures online looked divine. It had shiplap walls just like I adored and this rustic but modern feel to it. I was already half in love with it. And it was off the beach, but on the other side of the bay.

"Nonsense. That would be rude." Momma chastened me.

Do you know what's rude? Telling someone you love them in one breath and then walking away from them in the next. "I don't think he would mind."

"You were such good friends. I think it would mean a lot if you stayed." She laid on the guilt.

I wanted to say "were" was the operative word. As in past tense. Last time I saw him—before yesterday—he left me standing on the beach crying. But Momma was right, that was a long time ago. Even if sometimes it didn't feel like that. Maybe it was the sting of first love or perhaps the loss of a friend, a friend I always thought would be there. Either way, I could still feel the pain of it. I didn't dwell on it. I obviously moved on and chose another man who would leave me. Declan probably thought it was me that left him. I was only taking my parents' good advice to learn more about myself and to date more before I made such a huge commitment at eighteen. I wasn't trying to end us; I wanted to save us, if that made sense.

I sighed. "You win. Do you want me to set the table?"

She handed Daddy her spoon and made her way to me. She put her arm around my shoulder. "You're a good girl."

"Momma, I'm almost thirty."

She leaned her head against mine. "You will learn soon that your baby is always your baby. I love you. Now go set the table."

I smiled. "Inside or out?"

"It's such a beautiful day, let's eat on the veranda." She always put a little flair in when she pronounced veranda. She loved this three-story shingled-style home for the verandas on each level.

I loved it too, and the people in it. I needed them now more than ever. But I really needed to get my own place. And decide what to do with my life. I thought about opening my own financial planning firm. I didn't know if Indigo Bay would be the best place for that. I would probably have to look at the Charleston area. Did that mean I should buy a house in Charleston? I could rent, but I hated throwing money away.

My parents were all for me staying until after the baby was born. Decisions, decisions.

I took a moment to breathe in the sea air before I set the patio table for four. I still couldn't believe Declan was coming over. I looked over to my right at his old home. It stood about a thousand feet away. It was a darling two-story home in all white. I spent a lot of time over there and he over here. My parents always liked him. He was polite and would always offer to help Momma with anything from taking out the trash to filling the dishwasher. Momma used to say that someday he would make some lucky girl a good husband. She said it might even be me, but time would tell. She wanted us to take our time.

I stretched my lower back. I did that a lot lately. This baby seemed to camp out back there. I set the table, making sure to fold the linen napkins in the goblets like Momma liked. I walked through the sliding glass door in time to hear the doorbell ring. I took a deep breath and looked down at my linen shorts and navy chiffon blouse that showed off my baby bump that seemed to grow a little more each day. I didn't mind. It reminded me there were good things—the best things—to look forward to.

Daddy went to answer the door while I helped Momma put the finishing touches on the baked chicken and spring vegetables we were serving for lunch. It smelled fantastic. And Momma was all about the presentation, so it looked as good as it smelled. Even the water would be poured from a crystal pitcher. Her hostess skills she had passed down helped me as the wife of an executive. I could throw a good party if I had to. Thoughts for another time. I had to focus on the man walking in holding two bouquets of flowers.

His smile said he knew he was charming.

Momma fell for it hook, line, and sinker. She ran to him and hugged him, crushing the mixed bouquet and the violet tulips, my favorite, between them. "Declan, look at you." She barely reached the middle of his chest. She was shorter than me. "You're all grown up and looking so handsome."

He smiled at me before addressing Momma. "You don't look a day over thirty, Mrs. Dixon." Yep, he was a salesman, and a good one.

"Hey there, young fella, get your own girl." Daddy winked at me.

I resisted the urge to roll my eyes. Instead I turned to grab the platter full of food to take outside.

Declan rushed to my side with hands still full of flowers. "Let me get that."

"I've got it, thanks."

His blue eyes shined. And those lashes of his. He looked nice, too, in a short-sleeved button-up and shorts. He held out the violet tulips. "These are for you."

I wasn't sure what to do. I looked down at my full hands. I guess I could have set the platter down, but my brain wasn't functioning properly.

"Why don't we swap?" Declan suggested.

"How about," Daddy swooped in, "I take the food and you put those flowers in some water?"

How could I say no?

"Mrs. Dixon, these are for you." Declan handed Momma the pastel bouquet.

Momma kissed his cheek. "Always said you were a good catch. Melanie, darling, will you put these in a vase too and bring them out? We'll set them on the table."

I nodded and took her flowers. Declan still held mine.

"I'll help Mel." Declan announced.

My parents rushed out laughing as they went. I was beginning to think they were trying to set me up. Hello. I was recently divorced and pregnant. This was not a good time. And Declan…well, he had walked away.

"No need. I'll be out soon. You can lay those on the island." I turned from Declan to search for two vases.

"You used to say thank you when I brought you flowers."

I stopped and took a breath. He was right, and no matter our past I should at least use my manners. I turned and he was closer than before. His cologne hit me. Wow, he smelled good, warm and sensual. I had to step back. "Thank you." I peered into his eyes, which wasn't the best idea. Those baby blues were as beautiful and intoxicating as they used to be. I felt sixteen again, which was ridiculous. I was a pregnant mother-to-be. I stepped back even more.

He handed me the tulips. A smile played in his eyes. "I hope these are still your favorite."

I hesitated to take them. "You really shouldn't have."

He pushed them forward some more. "Why? We're old friends."

I turned from him without taking the flowers. "That's stretching the truth."

"Maybe we're not old." Levity marked his words.

"Or friends." I opened the cupboard that held some of Momma's vases.

"Ouch. I'm pretty sure you wrote 'best friends forever' in my yearbook."

I stood on my tiptoes to get the glass vase for Momma's flowers, carefully pulling it out and setting it on the granite countertop. I was pretty sure he wrote some things in mine too—things that he didn't mean. Like, I love you and something about me having the best body. He should see the tiny stretch marks I had going on. "Things change."

"Not everything." He handed me the flowers.

I took them and laid them next to Momma's bouquet. "Thank you. Why don't you join my parents? It's going to take me a few minutes to properly care for these."

"Perfect." He leaned against the counter and faced me. "We can catch up."

I sighed and pulled open a drawer near me looking for the kitchen scissors to trim the stems of the flowers.

"Looks like I'll be doing the talking." He edged closer.

I may have grinned.

"A smile. I can work that."

I didn't respond. I started trimming the stems. I knew better than to fall for his allure.

"You'll be happy to know I graduated from college. I have a great credit score. Still showering and brushing my teeth every day. I do admit sometimes I forget to floss, but I always do extra the next day. Never been arrested except for that one time in Mexico."

My head whipped toward him.

His smile said he knew he got to me. "I thought that might catch your attention."

I shook my head at him.

He scooted closer. "I've never been arrested. How about you?"

"What do you think?" I turned back to the flowers.

"I think you look great."

"I think you're obligated to say that."

"Obligated or not, it's true."

I inadvertently looked down at my midsection.

"Pregnancy suits you."

I looked up at him, he was somehow closer. "Why are you here?"

"Your dad invited me for lunch." He grinned.

"Why are you really here?"

He tugged on one of my curls. "I told you yesterday, I want to talk to you."

I focused back on the flowers and started to fill the vase.

"I know we didn't leave things on a good note." That was an understatement on his part.

I haphazardly began placing the flowers in the vase. I wanted to say, *well whose fault was that*, but like I said, I couldn't look back. I did it all too often without trying. "We were kids." I shoved the rest of the flowers in the vase and picked it up. I didn't need to be alone with him. He made me feel things—good and bad—that I didn't want to.

He touched my arm. "It didn't feel like that to me."

I remembered feeling grown up too. How wrong I was. I had and still have so much to learn, it seemed. I looked down at his hand on my arm. His touch felt so familiar, like a piece of me that had come home. "My parents are waiting."

He dropped his hand, but determination lingered in his eyes. "Let's not keep them."

Chapter Four

I COULDN'T HELP BUT STARE AT DECLAN SITTING ACROSS from me. It was like I had been transported back in time. My parents acted like no time had passed. They were as in love with him now as they had ever been. Momma couldn't get enough information out of him.

"Where are you staying? I hope nearby."

Declan wiped his mouth with his napkin. "I rented an apartment in Charleston off the river. Not sure where I will end up permanently."

"I do hope it's in Indigo Bay." Momma was laying it on thick. "Melanie's been looking at homes in the area, maybe you could look together." It was the first time she sounded happy about me moving out.

I picked up my glass of ice water to take a sip. "Momma, I'm sure Declan doesn't need my help."

Declan gave me a smile that should have been illegal before turning to Momma on his left. "That's a great idea, Mrs. D. No one knows the Bay better than her."

"It's settled then. You two kids always worked well together."

Uh, didn't I have a say? I looked at Daddy to intervene,

but as much as I had him wrapped around my finger, Momma enveloped him.

Daddy gave me a little wink. "When it comes to those things, a woman's opinion is much appreciated."

Declan lifted his glass. "Hear, hear."

Oh, I had some opinions. I narrowed my eyes at a smiling Declan. "You know I'm not even sure I'll be staying in Indigo Bay."

Momma swatted at me. "That's nonsense talk. Of course you will. Our baby needs to live close to me."

It was our baby, not my baby. I didn't mind. I loved that my parents loved this baby.

"When are you due?" Declan asked.

"End of July," Momma gushed, not letting me answer. "And tomorrow we find out if it's a boy or a girl."

Declan grinned at Momma's exuberance. He raised his glass one more time. "To Mel and the luckiest kid around." He was good. He had Momma tearing up and Daddy patting him on the back like a long-lost son. Even my little one did what felt like a somersault in response.

All I could do was give him a small smile and turn to my food. I wasn't sure what game he was playing, but I was obviously losing. That became more apparent as lunch wore on and he charmed my parents.

When we were eating our cake, he went in for the kill. "I was wondering, Mr. and Mrs. Dixon, if I could take Melanie for a walk—after I help with the dishes, of course." His Southern manners were out in full force, which was saying something for a man who had been raised as a Yankee. His family was originally from New York. And where did he get off asking my parents? I was a grown woman. I had been married and everything.

Momma placed her hand across her heart. "You are the sweetest thing alive. Don't worry about the dishes. Rich and I can take care of them. You kids enjoy your walk."

That's how I found myself walking out the lower-level patio door to the pool area with Declan. Glancing up at him I saw glimpses of the boy I used to know. He had a laid-back soul and was even tempered for the most part, with a few exceptions. One being the night I didn't accept his promise ring. His reaction surprised me. I thought he would have understood. I thought he knew how I felt about him.

We walked past the clear blue water of the pool. The waterfall gently rushed in the background. I admired the oasis our backyard was. Palm trees dotted the space, adding to the aura of it. I particularly loved the hammock that swung between two of them. It had been a favorite spot for the boy next door and me.

That boy was smiling over at me. "A lot of good memories happened here."

I put my hands in my pockets and nodded.

"Do you remember the welcome party you threw me?"

I did. I thought it would be nice if he got to know some people before school started, and admittedly, I wanted to check him out in swim trunks. I wasn't disappointed. Halle, Heather, and I all drooled over him. Looking at him now, I bet he would look even better. But I couldn't think about it.

"That was fun." I slipped off my shoes before we exited through the gate that led to the wooden pathway and past the dunes and beachy grass. I loved walking barefoot through the sand.

Declan opened the gate for us. "Why do I get the feeling you're only taking this walk with me to appease your parents?"

I met his eyes and sighed. "What did you expect after all this time?"

His lips pursed. "I don't know. I've wanted to talk to you for so long, but I never thought I would get the chance until yesterday. I didn't know you were back in town and ... divorced." He seemed embarrassed to add that last part.

"Did you even know I was married?"

The tips of his ears turned red. "Your mom sent my parents an announcement."

"Oh." I should have figured.

"You were a beautiful bride."

We sent announcements after the fact. Greyson wanted a quiet destination ceremony in Hawaii with only a few close friends and family. And it's not like we needed the typical newlywed gifts. Greyson was more than set. "Thanks." I bit my lip.

"You still bite your lip when you're nervous."

I gave him a small smile.

"Please just give me a few minutes of your time?"

His charm got to me. "I suppose I could spare a few minutes."

He grinned and closed the gate. We walked toward the almost uninhabited beach. The perks of living off a private beach, though once summer arrived it would become more crowded. For now it was just a dad with two of his daughters flying a kite in the spring air. Every time I saw children now, I thought about how that would be me soon. I was going to add flying a kite to the list of things I would teach this baby of mine.

Our walk was quiet until we were several yards from the house.

Declan looked at his old home as we walked in its direction, the wind breezing through our hair. "I thought my parents were ruining my life when they told me we were moving down here for my junior and senior year. Then you and your mom showed up with cookies."

I remember not wanting to go with her, but she insisted, and was I ever glad she did when Declan opened the door. It was instant attraction. Then the more I got to know him, I found him to be as beautiful on the inside as he was on the outside. Until he left me crying. I was over it, I really was. But being in his presence brought back the memories of the hurt. And I was still dealing with the disappointment of my failed marriage. At least Greyson's despicable actions didn't have me wondering what if, or pining for a lost love. Declan, on the other hand, had me wondering for a long time if I made the right decision. And I pined over him for longer than I cared to admit.

He looked out into the distance. "You made those some of the best years of my life."

"They were a lot of fun." Parties and bonfires on the beach, traveling together for cross country, proms and formals, kisses in the moonlight, sneaking out past curfew just to spend an hour more with him. There was a small cove a quarter mile down the beach where we would meet. We were headed that direction now.

"It was more than fun for me."

For me too.

He picked up a broken shell and examined it before tossing it into the ocean. "I guess what I'm trying to say is I'm sorry."

"For what?"

He stopped and I followed. His blue eyes owned mine. "You were right to reject my proposal." He let out a huge breath. "It took me a while to understand why and to see where you were coming from."

I studied him for a moment. He seemed relieved to get that off his chest. I turned back toward our walk, wondering how smart I really was.

"Does this mean I'm not forgiven?"

I shook my head. "Declan, it's been long forgiven."

"I wanted to tell you several years ago, but I wasn't sure you would ever want to see me again after the way we left things."

I pushed back his accusatory words of that night long ago. "I hurt and surprised you." I surprised even myself. "It's water under the bridge."

He grabbed my hand, and with that came a peaceful familiarity. It was shocking how good it felt. "Do you mean that?" His eyes pleaded in one breath, and turned playful in the next. "I mean, you will be my Realtor after all."

I pulled my hand away. It felt too comfortable in his. "I'm sure you can find your own place." I edged closer to the water and let the waves wash over my feet as I walked on the wet sand, letting it squish between my toes. The water was still cool this time of year, but bearable.

Declan kept in step with me. "It wouldn't be as much fun, though."

"I'm still not sure where I'll end up."

"Even better; we'll take our time and explore."

"I didn't say I needed your help."

"It's only fair, if you help me."

"I didn't say I would."

He nudged me. "You know you want to."

"For someone I haven't seen in almost twelve years, you're more than presumptuous. Don't you have a girlfriend that could help you out? Or your mom or sisters?"

"My parents are living in San Diego now, Colleen lives

in Dallas with her family, and Erica is currently overseas with her husband in Thailand. And I'm between girlfriends."

"What does that mean?"

"It means I don't have one."

That surprised me. "You could get a real Realtor."

"Come on, Mel. Are you going to make me beg?"

"I can send you some links."

"That's a start. You'll need my phone number and email." He pulled out his phone. "Just give me yours and I'll text you."

I leaned away and eyed him. The view wasn't bad at all. My baby kicked me, reminding me I was a mother-to-be and not some hormone-crazed teen admiring a lost love. I held my mid-section.

Declan followed my hand. "Are you all right?"

"Yes. It's the baby's favorite time of day to move."

His eyes filled with admiration. "Motherhood looks good on you."

"Now that I'm not puking every day, I love it."

"I can tell. Now give me your number."

"You're incorrigible."

"I can always get it from your mom."

She would definitely make sure he had it by the way she and Daddy were behaving. "Fine." I prattled off my number.

"This is the hardest I've ever had to work for a woman's number."

I'm sure he had women slipping him their number all the time.

We were almost to the cove. The place where it began and ended.

He noticed too. "Remember we used to race there?" There was a mixture of sweet and sorrow in his tone.

"You go ahead. I haven't run since I found out I was pregnant." The exhaustion mixed with vomiting and the turmoil left no energy for such things during the first trimester. Walking and swimming were my only forms of exercise now.

"I've already got my training in for the day."

"Training for what?"

"Spartan Races."

"What are those?"

"You've never heard of them?"

"Should I have?"

"I guess only the cool people know about them," he teased.

"I think if you are still using the word *cool*, it means you aren't."

"There's a little of the Mel I knew."

That Mel was long gone, replaced with the realistic version. "So are you going to enlighten me?"

"I thought I would keep you in suspense a little bit longer." He was still his lighthearted self.

A smile escaped.

"I missed your smile." That didn't sound lighthearted at all. It sounded like regret.

"You aren't the only one." I missed my smile too.

"I'm sorry for whatever you've been through." He focused on my baby bump.

I wondered how much Daddy told him about my divorce. "Don't be. It was all for the best. Now tell me about these Spartan Races." We needed to change the subject. I had this urge to bare my soul to him and it was discomforting. The connection I had always felt with him crept up to the surface. It had from the first day we'd met, but I figured it would be long gone.

The light brightened in his eyes. "They're obstacle races. The last one I did was eight miles long with over twenty-five obstacles."

"What kind of obstacles are we talking about?"

"You know, crawling under live barbed-wire, carrying fifty-pound sandbags up and down huge flights of stairs, scaling cliffs without harnesses—"

"Are you teasing me?"

"No, ma'am."

"You do this for fun?"

"Yeah, and to stay in shape. My next race is in a few weeks in North Carolina."

"Wow. Good for you."

"Spectators can come."

"Is that so?"

"I just thought I'd throw that out there." His smile warmed me up in a way I hadn't felt in a very long time.

Chapter Five

∾

I SAT ON THE CANOPY BED IN MY PARENTS' GUEST BEDROOM late that night flipping through my yearbook from senior year. Declan's presence was bringing back all sorts of forgotten memories. At almost thirty years old, I felt silly reliving my high school days, especially under my not so auspicious circumstances. But there I was, staring at photos of my first love with the ocean waves and jazz for background music.

There we were on the cross country page standing next to each other for the team picture. We looked like babies. He really had grown up. And did I ever have skinny legs. I ran my hand down my shapelier bare legs. I think I liked the ones I had now better. I liked the way Declan had filled out too.

I turned to the prom pictures. We were one of the couples captured. He looked handsome in his black tux as he held me close on the dance floor. I loved that red off-the-shoulder gown. Momma probably had it around here somewhere. Not like I was getting into it. I noted the way my head rested on his shoulder and how the camera caught his expression. He looked at me as if he held everything.

I don't think Greyson ever felt that way, or even knew how to.

Case in point, the tulips that Momma placed on my nightstand next to my bed. I guess she thought they deserved to be preserved and displayed. You see, after all these years, Declan remembered those were my favorite flowers. Greyson never once asked what my favorites were, and even when I mentioned it, he glossed over it. And he never brought or sent me "just because" flowers. I only got flowers after an argument. Those arguments usually surrounded things like him forgetting my birthday, or all the time he spent at the office. His way of saying sorry was to buy me something, and if it was flowers, it was large bouquets of red roses. I only wanted his time. I wanted him to look at me like I was his everything. That's how I felt about him. Not anymore. He used me and I was too blind to see it.

But I could never regret my relationship with him. Not now that I carried with me the best gift I had ever been given. Greyson was what Momma called one of those sweet regrets life gave us. Her outlook was that others may disappoint us or we may even disappoint ourselves, but there was always something to learn from our mistakes, so there lies the sweetness.

The baby stirred, bringing me out of my thoughts about my ex-husband. I flipped to the back pages where Declan signed my book. His scribbly handwriting took up a whole page. I read through it and actually teared up some as he shared his heart with me. He said some of the same things he said tonight, like I made his junior and senior years the best. How ridiculous I was being. And what did he know, professing his undying love for me? He was eighteen. And not too long after those words were written he would accuse me of only wanting to see other people and that I lied about my feelings for him.

He was wrong.

I closed the book and lay back on the several pillows I now needed every night to keep my pregnant body comfortable. I looked around at the gorgeous room with white bedding and flowy curtains that swayed along with the sea breeze. The dark wood played off it well. It was a romantic room, which made me feel more alone. I didn't miss Greyson. Mostly. There were some good memories at the beginning. I wouldn't have married him in the first place if there wasn't. But the bed felt lonely. One thing I will give him was he came home every night and held me. Sometimes it was the only time during the day I had him to myself. It was the reason I never suspected he was cheating on me and why I convinced myself he loved me. I didn't think a man would behave in such a way if he didn't.

I needed to quit thinking about men. My focus was my baby. I was excited to finally know for sure it was a girl. I just had this feeling. And I was dying to start buying everything. So was Momma. She didn't do doctors' offices, but she knew her way around a shopping center and she was itching to spend some serious money on her grandchild.

With that thought I turned off my bedside lamp and snuggled in under the comforter. I rested my hand on my baby and fell asleep.

౷

I crossed my legs, waiting for the ultrasound tech. "I've never had to pee so bad in my life."

Halle and Heather both laughed.

"You guys have no idea. They made me drink a quart of water before I came in. And I swear this little one uses my bladder as a bed. Now it's like a waterbed and she's jumping on it."

"Could be a he," Heather reminded me.

I hadn't forgotten, but I was sure it was a little girl. I was going to name her Lillian Maria Dixon. Lillian for my grandmother and Maria after Momma.

Halle lowered her thick framed glasses that she only wore as an accessory, she had great eye sight. "You never told us what happened at lunch yesterday with Declan."

"Ooo, yeah." Heather put down the breastfeeding pamphlet.

I shrugged. "Not much to tell. We ate and talked."

"The question is, what did you talk about? And was it the kind that didn't involve words?" Heather laughed at herself.

"Why would you think that?"

She gave an innocent shrug. "I don't know, maybe because all you guys did back in high school was make out. And let's not forget how fine he looks now. Or that you're glowing and have always had this come hither look to you."

"Please. Don't make me laugh. I mean that. I might wet my pants." And don't get me thinking about the way he kissed. He was a natural and I had never met his equal. And that's saying something.

They both laughed for me.

"You didn't deny that you kissed," Halle pointed out.

"I thought it would be obvious that we didn't. We haven't seen each other in forever, and we were children, and now I'm having one. And I'm so over men."

They looked between themselves, speaking their twin language. "Uh-huh."

"Declan is my past."

"So you aren't going to see him again?" Halle seemed disappointed.

I bit my lip. "Well…"

They both leaned in eager.

"Momma suggested that I help him look for a place to live. And he invited me to watch him run a Spartan Race."

"I've heard of those." Heather's eyes lit up. "Take me; those races attract some seriously hot men."

"I'm not going."

"Why ever not?" Heather looked at me like I was crazy.

Halle looked up to the ceiling and sighed. "I'm wondering if it still isn't kismet. The universe may be trying to speak to you."

"She's telling me I need to pee."

And thankfully that's when the ultrasound tech walked in. "Hi, I'm Cleo." She looked so young. Like middle-school young. Except her tattooed arms said she was at least eighteen, so that was good. I could tell Halle was digging Cleo's pink hair and combat boots. Maybe Halle would go pink next.

Cleo, despite her young looks, was professional. She helped me lay on the exam table and went right to work. She squeezed some warm blue gel on my bare abdomen, which didn't help with the having to pee thing, but it was worth it once the transducer connected with my skin and my world appeared on the screen near me. Tears poured down my face.

Halle and Heather each stood on a side and took a hand. We were all entranced watching my little one move inside of me.

Everything I had been through the past several months faded away in an instant. All that mattered was the beautiful baby on the screen.

Cleo measured and pointed out the baby's heart and liver. She counted all the baby's fingers and toes. They were all there.

"She's so beautiful," Halle commented. "I may rethink having one of my own."

Cleo cleared her throat. "You did want to know the sex, right?"

"Yes," we all answered eagerly.

Cleo grinned and pointed out what was clearly the type of thing that landed me in my current position. "You're beautiful she is a he."

My best friends squeezed my hands.

"A boy." I wasn't expecting that, but it didn't matter. He was going to be the most loved son ever. And he would be better than the sperm donor ever was. And with any luck he would look like me. Not that his "father" wasn't attractive— he was gorgeous, with dark tousled hair and gray eyes—but when my son looked at me I wanted him to see himself, because I knew the day would come when he would ask why he didn't have a father. And it killed me to think of Greyson's selfishness and his signing away any rights he had to my son. How was I going to explain that?

Thoughts for another day. Today was nothing but a joyous occasion. I was having a son.

It took Cleo about twenty minutes to do her thing. My friends and I stared at the monitor in amazement for the duration. It wasn't until Cleo left that my friends made mention about the surprise.

"Are you sure you're okay?" Halle patted my cheeks. She was the touchy feely one.

"I'm happy, more than happy. Except, I really have to pee. Can you ladies meet me in the exam room?" Cleo had let me know which room Dr. Winters would see me in for my regular appointment. We would also discuss the ultrasound there. My friends wanted to be part of the whole experience since this was something new for all of us. And I had nothing to hide from them.

On the way to the bathroom I stared at the black and white pictures of my son that Cleo had printed off. He was perfect. There was even one of him sucking his thumb. It was the sweetest thing ever. I loved this baby with all that I was.

I swore I peed for ten minutes. Holding all that water was tortuous. A man had to have come up with that bright idea. While washing my hands, I saw some light in my hazel eyes. They were more green than they had been. That was a good sign. I felt like I was finally walking out of a dark tunnel back into the sunshine.

And I wasn't the only one feeling good. I walked into the exam room to already find Dr. Noah Winters, aka Dr. Of Every Woman's Dream, flirting with my best friends. Or was it them flirting with him? For the record, I wasn't attracted to him. Yes, he was good looking, but he was nothing compared to, let's say, Declan, for the sake of argument. The doctor was a pretty boy; blonde hair and blue eyes, but not Declan blue. Dr. Winters had pale blue eyes. Declan was ruggedly handsome with eyes as deep and blue as I had ever seen. His eyes told a story of how good he was. Dr. Winters eyes said, I know I'm good. Big difference. But he was one of the most sought-after OB-GYN's in the area.

Dr. Winters was like a coach. He would jump up on the counter in the exam room and talk to you about the game plan. There he was on the counter regaling a harrowing tale of how he had to deliver twins in a car on the side of the highway once. My best friends sat there enthralled with doe eyes. I had never seen such behavior from Halle. It didn't surprise me to see Heather tossing her hair and licking her lips, but Halle sat in a trance. Dr. Winters wasn't her type. She liked the hipsters or the men that turned up their noses on careers like doctors or lawyers. She would have rather been with a starving artist or author. But there in her brown eyes I saw her willingness to throw her ideals out the door. Unfortunately, Heather had the same hungry eyes. They had never liked the same man before.

I was hoping Dr. Winters was already taken and this wouldn't be an issue.

I cleared my throat.

Dr. Winters finally took notice of me. He clapped his hands and jumped off the counter. "Sorry. I get carried away sometimes. Why don't you have a seat on the table." He kindly helped me up.

My friends looked jealous when he touched me.

While Dr. Winters pulled up my ultrasound results on the computer in the room, Heather pretended to fan herself. Halle looked discouraged. She knew Heather was on the prowl, and we both knew she always got her man.

I felt bad for Halle. She saw herself in the shadows of Heather's beauty, though she was as beautiful as her sister. I think sometimes that's why she did crazy things with her hair, it was her way of standing out. I loved it and at times wished I was brave enough to try something like it, but I was chicken. I loved Halle's quiet confidence and Heather's zeal.

I would have to worry about my friends' obvious attraction for my doctor later. I was eager to hear what he had to say about my baby, my son. I had to get used to that.

Dr. Dreamy flashed me his dazzling capped-tooth smile. "Everything is looking good. His organs look normal and are developing properly. We may be a little off on the due date. You are measuring a week ahead of schedule. That's not a big deal. We can move up your due date."

That was exciting news and not all that unexpected. Since I had been taking the pill, I wasn't exactly sure when I had conceived. And Greyson and I had a healthy physical relationship. Like I said, he didn't have a reason to cheat. But I read somewhere that sometimes when they make love to you more often than normal, that's a sign. They do it out of guilt. I couldn't think now about how little that made me feel.

Dr. Winters did his own exam, but the kind I liked—the external kind. I knew toward the end of my pregnancy it would be the invasive kind. He poked and prodded my bare abdomen. My little guy moved around accordingly. I loved the feel of him. I needed to come up with a name for him.

Dr. Winters found everything to be satisfactory. He helped me into an upright position. "Let's see you in three weeks, you'll be twenty-eight weeks then. Make sure to have your birth plan filled out for next time. We'll go over that. We'll also do your glucose test to check for gestational diabetes."

That wasn't good news. I heard it was awful. I nodded in acknowledgment. I had already been filling out my birth plan and I was looking at birthing classes.

"Any questions?"

"I don't think so."

"Keep doing what you're doing. The goal line's in sight." There was his coach talk. Before leaving he looked at his new admirers, otherwise known as my friends. "You ladies have a great day." I think I heard the ting from his flashy smile, just like in the movies.

I watched my friends melt into a puddle of goo. I shook my head at them.

We all walked out together. Dr. Winters went left and we went right so I could check out. I should say I went right.

I had to drag my friends away.

"I'm getting his number," Heather whispered. I think she was oblivious to Halle's feelings.

Halle's eyes fell as she watched Heather chase down Dr. Winters. I had to give it to Heather, she wasn't afraid to go after what she wanted.

I strung my arm through Halle's. "I want to hire you to decorate the nursery."

She stood up straighter, trying not to act disappointed. "At your parents' place?"

"No. I've decided I need to get my own home. Not sure where, but I'm going to get serious about house hunting."

"I hope you stay in the Bay."

"That's my parents' hope as well. And I would love for this little guy to grow up there, but Charleston may make more sense depending on my job situation."

"Where's Declan going to settle?" She grinned.

"Why does that matter?"

"All I'm saying is *kismet*."

"What if I don't believe in fate?"

"You don't have to. It believes in you."

Chapter Six

I WANTED TO TELL DADDY IN PERSON THAT HE WAS GET-ting a grandson. I already called Momma and she was beside herself happy. I wouldn't be surprised if I came home to find every item from Babies"R"Us in the living room. I stopped at a baby boutique near the medical district in Charleston close to Daddy's office. I bought the cutest little outfits and a shirt for Daddy that read, "Grandpa and Grandson, Best Friends for Life." Daddy was going to be tickled.

This was all turning out different than I imagined, but I was determined to make it okay. This little boy would be more than loved. I just needed to come up with a name for him. I could name him after Daddy and Grandad, Richard Landry Dixon. But that seemed outdated. I would have to keep thinking about it. Maybe I should Google popular boy names. I did know one name for sure he would never have, and that was Greyson Ellis III. If only Greyson knew I was having a boy, or his mother. She more than anyone wanted that name to live on. It was, after all, her late husband's. I never met the man. From all accounts, he was wonderful—unlike his son. There I went thinking about him again. I supposed it was natural, but I wanted to forget that my ex-husband ever existed.

I took my purchases and wrapped gift for Daddy and headed his way. I hadn't been to his office since I'd been home. I'd spent the first month just trying to readjust and deal with the repercussions of my divorce.

I pulled into the parking lot of Dixon Construction and smiled. I loved the vintage red-brick building that looked like a throwback to days gone by, even if it was only five years old. Daddy was so proud when he completed what he called his favorite project. He liked to call it the corporate office. He mostly spent his days in trailers on different construction sites.

My phone vibrated. I pulled it out of my purse, figuring it was Momma again asking me some baby related question. I wasn't sure why. I had no idea what I was doing yet or exactly what I needed. But it wasn't Momma.

What's the verdict?

Verdict? I was confused by Declan's question and why he was texting me in the middle of the day for no reason. He texted me last night so I would have his info, since Momma volunteered me to help him find a place. I didn't assume it would go beyond that, unless that's what he meant by verdict. If he thought I already found a place for him, he was sorely mistaken.

Girl or boy?

Oh. *Boy.* That was nice of him to ask.

Congratulations.

Thank you.

When can we house hunt? I'm available this week in the evenings and the weekend. Or both.

He was pushing it. *Let me check my schedule.* Not like I really had one. Except I needed to sign up for some birthing and breastfeeding classes. And I could think up some other stuff. I'm sure Halle was going to want to hang out now that

Heather had a date with my doctor. I wasn't sure how to feel about that. I made a request that I never see him outside the office. And anything regarding my pregnancy never be discussed between the two.

I grabbed the gift for Daddy and headed in. I waved a hello to Danielle, who was on the phone. She had been Daddy's receptionist since forever. I think she was a grandma now herself. I admired the plank flooring and bricked walls as I walked back. For a construction office, it had charm.

Daddy too was on the phone. His eyes lit up when he saw me. He held his finger up and gave me a wink, telling me to hold on. It sounded like he was arguing with a subcontractor about the Bellvue building. I looked at his mess of a desk and smiled. He really needed to hire a new office manager. He had been without one for a couple of months.

My phone buzzed again. I pulled it out of my bag.

Let me take you to dinner this week to celebrate. We can go over listings then.

I stared at my phone, not sure how to respond.

"Darlin'," Daddy interrupted my dilemma.

I smiled up at him.

"What's got you consternated?"

I threw my phone in my bag. "Nothing. It's just Declan asking me to have dinner with him."

Daddy's smile engulfed his face. "I like that boy. He's grown up to be a fine man and one heck of a sales guy. He convinced me to use Redline for the Lawrence building on Sycamore."

"Why is he handling it? Doesn't Redline have territory managers?"

"You're a smart cookie and so is he. He's using his personal connection."

That made sense. But Declan was distracting me from the real reason I came. I held up my craft paper package. "Let's forget about Declan for a moment. I have something for you."

Daddy met me in front of his desk. "I've been waiting for you to call." He kissed my cheek.

"I wanted to tell you in person." I handed him the neatly tied package.

"You've always been my favorite daughter."

I grinned as I watched him open the gift. Then my eyes welled up with tears as he read the shirt and moisture appeared in his own.

He was so choked up, he couldn't speak. Instead he pulled me in for a bear hug.

And there I stayed for several minutes. I reveled in the comfort only a daddy could give. "I take it you're happy."

"Baby girl, I haven't been this happy since your momma told me she was pregnant with you." He kissed the top of my head. "We are going to celebrate tonight. I'm calling Willis' to make reservations. And then I'm going to buy my grandson a pony or something."

I laughed against his chest. "Daddy, where would you put a horse?"

"I'll buy some property."

"I think Momma's already planning to buy out the baby store, so let's hold off on any large animals."

He gave me another squeeze before he let go to make the reservations at the finest steak house in Charleston. It overlooked the river. "The Dixon name will live on."

I knew how important that was to him. It's why I kept it as my middle name when I got married, but I promptly took it back as my last name as soon as I was divorced. I knew

Daddy would never say it, but he was sad they could never have more children. He always made me feel like a princess, but I don't think he would have minded a prince. And now we were going to have one.

Daddy picked up his phone, a sly grin playing on his lips. "You know, Declan lives near Willis'."

My eyes narrowed. "I remember him mentioning something about living near the river."

"Then it's settled. Invite him to dinner tonight."

"Daddy?"

"What, darlin'? He already asked you to dinner. It would be rude not to invite him."

"I don't see how."

"Just take your old man's word for it." He dialed the restaurant's number.

I pulled out my own phone.

Declan had texted again. *I'll chew with my mouth closed and everything. Don't leave me hanging.*

I grinned and sighed. I justified my response with the argument that we were only friends. He even said last night that's all he wanted from me. And I could use more friends right now. *How about dinner tonight with my parents at Willis'. Does six work for you?*

Can't wait.

I wasn't sure how to feel about it.

❦

Momma and I drove into Charleston together to meet Daddy and now Declan for dinner.

"Karen has already said she wants to throw a baby shower for you." Karen was Momma's best friend.

"I don't need one." I didn't want the attention.

"Nonsense. Everyone is expecting there to be one."

I wasn't. "Um…okay, but only a small gathering." I knew Momma and her friend would do it with or without my blessing, so I thought I should stipulate. Not that it would do much good, but I could try.

Momma smiled like I could live in my make-believe world. She already had a plan by the looks of her impish grin.

"Please nothing over the top."

She reached over and patted my bare knee while I drove. "It will be perfect, as will my baby."

I gave her a small smile.

"And I can't tell you how happy I am that Declan is join-ing us tonight. I always hoped you two kids would find a way back to each other."

If I could have grabbed my heart I would have. "Momma, why would you say that?"

"Why wouldn't I? He's as good as gold and now you're old enough."

"I'm not looking for a relationship. I'm barely out of my failed marriage."

From the corner of my eye I could see her face scrunch in furious fashion. "You did not fail. It was Greyson that flunked out." She said his name with such vehemence. Once upon a time she loved him, which made her hate him even more now.

"Regardless, I can't entertain a relationship with anyone right now."

She stroked my hair that somewhat behaved itself tonight. It looked unruly on purpose at least. "You didn't deserve any of this, and I'm so proud of the way you've handled it all."

She had me tearing up. "I'm just putting one foot in front of the other."

"You don't have to do it alone."

"I have you and Daddy."

"As much as we love you, it isn't the same as a partner."

That was true, but…"How can I ever trust myself or another man again?"

"It will come, just don't close yourself off to it."

"Momma, all I need now are friends."

"Friends to lovers are the best kinds of relationships." She sighed like a much younger woman.

"You aren't going to let this go, are you?"

"All I'm saying, honey, is I saw the way he looked at you during lunch yesterday, and he's as enthralled with you as he ever was."

"Maybe you need to get your contact prescription checked."

She smacked my arm. "I'm not the blind one here."

Between my family and my friends, I was going to have to stay away from Declan. I didn't need anyone getting the wrong impression. I was a mother-to-be for goodness sake. And could we all please remember we were teenagers when we dated? Our lives are completely different now, other than I was living with my parents. For all we knew we wouldn't get along as adults. Though I had a hard time believing that. Declan seemed to be as charming as he ever was.

Let's face it, the man showed up to dinner with a gift for the baby.

We were already seated when he came strolling in holding a blue giftbag with tissue paper popping out of it. Not many men would add the frivolity. And did I mention how handsome he looked? My guess was that he went home and changed. He was wearing dark trousers and a crisp blue button-up that looked like a million bucks on him. I was glad

Momma suggested I wear the white eyelet sundress. Not like I needed to impress him, but now I didn't look underdressed next to him. Because of course that's exactly where my parents wanted him to sit.

Daddy stood up to greet Declan with a handshake.

"I'm sorry I'm a few minutes late." He ran his hand through his damp hair. He definitely went home to change.

"No worries at all, we were barely seated." Momma smiled up at him.

Declan kissed her cheek in greeting.

I think Momma blushed.

Without warning, Declan also kissed my cheek. "You look beautiful, congratulations." He handed me the bag before he took his seat.

I touched my cheek with one hand and held the bag in the other. I hadn't received much to any affection or compliments from men other than Daddy in a long time. I told myself it was friendly as he had done the same to Momma, but the way he was staring at me didn't seem all that platonic. In fact, it warmed me in a way I hadn't felt in too long. "Thank you," I remembered to say.

"You're welcome. Open it."

All eyes were focused on me as I removed the tissue paper and pulled out a dark blue baby wrap. I had been wanting one so I could carry my little guy around when the time came. "This is so thoughtful. Thank you." I studied the packaging.

"I called my sister and she suggested it. She said this was the best one on the market. She used one for her last baby."

I placed the gift back in the bag and met Declan's eyes. I wanted to say something to convey how touched I was, but Momma got to him before I could. She grabbed his hand.

"You are the sweetest man ever."

"Hey now, what about me?" Daddy laughed.

In the midst of my parents' banter, Declan's eyes fixed on me for a few seconds longer. In them I saw the boy who made my toes curl and heart pound. It was good when he turned away and addressed my parents. "I'm sure Mr. Dixon has me beat."

Momma rested her hand on top of Declan's. "We are going to keep you around."

Declan faced me. "I sure hope so."

I had to turn away. I wasn't ready to feel the things stirring within me.

The waiter came at the perfect moment. Food was a good thing to focus on. He listed their specials, took our drink order, and let us be. Daddy ordered a bottle of wine for everyone besides me, of course. I would be sticking with good old water with lemon. Though I felt like I had drunk more than my fair share of water for the day. My bladder was still recovering from the earlier excruciating pain. But my stomach was ready for steak, au gratin potatoes, and grilled asparagus.

"So have you thought of names?" Declan perused his menu.

That piqued my parents' interest.

"A few, but I haven't chosen one. I thought for sure this baby was a girl."

"I told you." Daddy gave me a wink.

"Yes, you did." I smiled back at him.

"You know, Richard is a good strong name," Daddy put his plug in, making Declan and Momma laugh.

"It is." I wasn't going to commit to anything. I didn't want to get his hopes up.

"You could always name him Mel, after you," Declan suggested.

"I don't think he would appreciate that as he got older."

"True," Declan agreed.

"At least we already know what he'll be when he grows up," Daddy surprised me.

I gave Daddy my full attention. He was beaming. "And what's that?"

"He'll own Dixon Construction once you pass it down to him."

I tilted my head. "I didn't know I was inheriting it."

Daddy sat up business like. "I was hoping this dinner could be more than just a celebration for the baby. I want you to come work for me. Take on an executive roll, learn the ropes. I need a smart financial mind like yours."

I sat back in shock. I hadn't ever considered the possibility.

"You can bring the baby to work," Daddy sweetened the deal.

"Or I'll watch him," Momma eagerly volunteered.

Daddy's eyes owned mine. He was dead serious. "Think about it, baby girl."

I nodded. "I will." Wow. How unexpected, but not unwelcome. It kind of excited me, but I knew I should think about it before making such a huge commitment.

After that everything else seemed to be a blur. I listened and participated in the conversations, but I kept thinking about Daddy's offer, or when Declan's hand brushed mine on occasion. The fluttering in my mid-section was not the baby, though he moved too. That never got old.

I was so lost in my thoughts I found myself absentmindedly agreeing to a stroll down the Riverwalk with Declan.

This night was full surprises.

Chapter Seven

꿍

"ARE YOU GOING TO TAKE YOUR DAD UP ON HIS OFFER?"

I turned my gaze from the lights reflecting off the river to the handsome man walking next to me. "That's a good question. I'm seriously considering it."

"You acted so surprised. Didn't you assume you would eventually take it over?"

"Honestly no. Greyson—. You know, never mind."

"Is Greyson your ex-husband?"

"Yes, but I try not to think about him. He never would have wanted a life here. And our life centered around his life, so no, I never thought about Dixon Construction being mine."

"So, Miss Dixon, what do you think now?"

I took a deep breath and smiled. "I think I want some ice cream." There was a cute shop up ahead that made their own ice cream.

He laughed deep into the warm spring air. "Your wish is my command."

A bell rang as we entered the shop. There were only a few other patrons in the quaint little place. I looked at their handwritten menu on a chalkboard sign.

"Is strawberry still your favorite?" Declan seemed to only have eyes for me.

"Yes, but the baby seems to love chocolate."

"You can do a scoop of both."

"Good thinking." I did just that on a sugar cone.

Declan got one scoop of nonfat peach frozen yogurt in a cup.

"You know you're making me look bad." We stood at the counter waiting for our dessert.

"I don't think that's possible."

I nudged him. "Thank you for everything tonight. The gift, the walk, the ice cream." He had insisted on paying.

"It's my pleasure, but I hope our walk isn't over."

"It can't be now. I have to pretend to burn off some of these calories." I took the cone bursting with two large scoops.

"You actually look like you need a few extra." His eyes said he was concerned.

"I'm okay. It's been a rough few months, but I'm better."

He gave my free hand a quick squeeze. "I'm glad."

His touch warmed me. "Me too." And I was glad I had someone to enjoy the beautiful spring night with. Flowers lined our path, the scent of jasmine and the nearby restaurants hung in the air. It was serene and Declan's company only made it that much better. Not to mention the scrumptious ice cream.

"You know, my office isn't that far away from your dad's."

"Are you trying to talk me into taking the job?"

He grinned over at me. "I'm just saying we could do lunch on occasion."

"I don't know a lot about the construction world. That was always Daddy's thing."

"I can help you there too."

"I'm sure you have better things to do with your time. Like burpees." He had told me last night if you couldn't complete a certain obstacle in the Spartan Races, you had to do a certain number of burpees to continue. It sounded awful.

He chuckled. "There hasn't been an obstacle I haven't been able to conquer yet."

"Well, color me impressed. Then I'm sure you have lots of training to do."

"I'd make time for you. Besides you're helping me find a place. I owe you."

Which reminded me of some things I should ask. "Do you really want to live in Indigo Bay, or would Charleston be better for you? Do you want a house or a condo?"

"It depends." He took a bite of his frozen yogurt.

"On what?"

He took a moment and swallowed. "Stuff."

"What kind of stuff?"

"Stuff I'm working on."

I narrowed my eyes at him. "Are you trying to be mysterious or annoying?"

He wagged his eyebrows. "I can do both."

I shook my head at him and turned back to my ice cream. The baby's somersaults indicated he liked it too. "You never did tell me why you came back here."

He shrugged between bites. "Job."

"That's all? It's a far cry from where you were in Tennessee."

He looked out over the water. "I love it here. Out of all the places I've lived, this is the one place that always comes to mind." He faced me. "Some of my best memories were here."

I bit my lip. "You did take state in cross country."

His deep blue eyes flooded mine. "The only thing I remember about that day is you standing at the finish line, and kissing you on the bus once it was dark enough not to get caught."

I remembered that day too. The feel of being held against his sweat-soaked body when he picked me up and swung me around. The stolen kisses that I never seemed to get enough of at the time. "That was a good day." I turned from him. I had no business feeling anything but friendship for him.

"I plan on making more good memories here." It was as if he was giving me fair warning.

∽∾∽

Declan kept running through my mind even as I looked at fabric and paint swatches for the baby's room at H2O the next day. I knew I should get a place first, but I couldn't resist the urge. And I felt like I should be there for Halle in case she wanted to talk. Besides, I loved hanging out at their place. The décor had a soothing affect. The main area was painted in a color named Harmonious, which perfectly described the light blue with a hint of green. It complemented the large white H2O sign on the main wall and white mismatched furniture that matched, if that made sense. It was shabby chic at its best and totally Halle and Heather.

Halle sat down next to me, adding a new book of pictures to scroll through to the pile we had on the table in the middle of the open office space. "Do you have a theme in mind?"

I pulled up a picture on my phone. Daddy got me thinking yesterday when he talked about buying my little guy a pony. "I love this rocking horse."

Halle's eyes lit up and I could see her mind fill with a hundred ideas as she studied the beautiful hand-carved horse I found online and ordered late last night. She handed my phone back and shot up. She ran to her desk and grabbed a sketch pad. In no time, she was sketching out a masterpiece.

"Are you doing okay?" I watched her, mesmerized by her ability.

She kept her eyes on her drawing. "You mean because my sister is having lunch with your doctor?" She pressed a little too hard with her pencil and broke the lead.

I took the pencil out of her hand. "You should have said something to Heather."

She met my eyes and sighed. "I don't even know why I'm attracted to him."

"He's handsome."

"He's okay."

I tilted my head. "What do you mean by that?"

She shrugged. "I know Heather thinks he's gorgeous, most women probably do, but it was more the way he talked and his bedside manner. And when he walked into the room before you got there, he looked at me first and smiled. That never happens when Heather and I are together."

"She'll probably get bored with him."

"You didn't hear her talking about him this morning. She's always wanted to date a doctor. And now that you're pregnant, her biological clock is ticking louder than ever. And I don't want her leftovers. And there's the sister code."

"I'm sorry, Hal."

She waved me off and took back her pencil. "It's fine. It would have never worked anyway. He's too pretty for my taste."

"He is kind of shiny."

She laughed. "That's a good word for him." She grabbed a new pencil from her case. "So, what's going on with you and Declan?"

"Nothing." I focused on the paint samples in front of me.

"Uh-huh. Try again."

"Really. We're friends."

"You guys have never been only friends. Even before you started dating you could tell there was a connection between you that went deeper than friendship."

I looked up into her wise eyes. "I know."

"Do you think he still has feelings for you?"

"I'm carrying another man's child. I think that's a turn off for most men."

"Do you want him to be turned on by you?" She grinned.

"No."

"You're lying."

I played with my curls. "I can't think like that. I have a baby coming, and what we shared was young love. And I have a terrible track record with adult relationships."

"Love is love. It wasn't that long ago that many girls married right out of high school. Not that I think it's a good idea, but lots of those marriages endured. And you aren't responsible for Greyson's actions. If he was a better man you would still be married." She was always the voice of reason.

"How will I ever know who is a good man? I thought Greyson and Declan were. Both men left me crying."

She thought for a moment, tapping her pencil against her pad. "The world isn't made up of good people and bad people. Everyone is some of both—some more than others. You wouldn't have married Greyson if he wasn't a 'good' person. But he made some terrible mistakes. The kind of mistakes that change the course of lives. The kind you typically can't come back from. The kind a man of his age should know better than to make. Declan on the other hand, made a hotheaded assumption. And to be fair, our brains don't fully attach until we're twenty-five. He was eighteen."

A small laugh escaped. "Is that a scientific fact?"

"It is." She went back to drawing.

"I don't have any room right now in my life for regret."

"Maybe, but you could regret walking away from a second chance."

Chapter Eight

I AGREED TO MEET DECLAN ON SATURDAY TO HOUSE HUNT and have lunch with him at Sweet Caroline's. It probably wasn't the smartest move. I knew how the tongues would wag, but it was only a matter of time before the rumor mill started now that he and I were back in the area. I was sure the odd coincidence was going to be seen by some as anything but coincidental.

I arrived early. Momma was driving me crazy with her talk of Declan. She couldn't quit gushing about him. She would have had him over every night had I not talked her out of it. That wasn't to say there wasn't a part of me that looked forward to seeing him, but I was doing my best to tell that part it wasn't a good idea. We had other things to worry about. Like me starting my new job on Monday. Daddy was persuasive. He even sent me an official offer. It was more than generous. I was going to be the CFO. It was a fancier title than I had ever held, though I wasn't sure how much it counted since Daddy bestowed it upon me. Nepotism was alive and well at Dixon Construction. But at least it was a new position. I didn't take it from anyone, though I'm sure it would be ruffling some feathers.

I was looking forward to going back to work. I had said goodbye to the financial planning firm I worked for in Philadelphia several weeks ago when I moved back to Indigo Bay. I owed so much to my coworkers and boss there. They had kept me going in the midst of my divorce saga and morning sickness. The women I worked with would bring me crackers every morning and cover for me when I was puking my guts out in the bathroom. It was a rough few months all around. I cried myself to sleep every night curled up in a ball on the couch. I couldn't sleep in the lonely bed. I felt betrayed beyond anything I could have ever imagined.

But health and happiness were returning. Going back to work was a step in the right direction. And getting my own place.

I grabbed the couch at Sweet Caroline's. My body appreciated it over the stiff chairs. I smiled as I watched Miss Caroline serve pie and advice. She was like Dear Abby, but better because you got real time answers. I listened to her talk to Florence Taylor, who obviously was desperate to get her boyfriend of ten years to pop the question.

"Honey, you need to go cold turkey. He has strung you out for far too long. We are all talking about it."

Florence dabbed her eyes.

"You deserve better." Miss Caroline placed a slice of her award-winning boysenberry pie on the table in front of her.

It was as if everyone around agreed with Miss Caroline. They were nodding and crossing their hearts for the poor soul.

I myself wanted to yell at her to run as far away as she could and never look back. Instead I smiled at Miss Caroline shaking her head and muttering, "Bless her heart."

I caught Miss Caroline's eyes. "Well, I'll be. Look at you. I've been hoping I would see you in here. I hear I missed you last time you were in. It seems like yesterday you were in high school." Miss Caroline focused on my baby bump. "And look at you darlin', you're glowing."

I appreciated that she didn't make mention of my ex-husband or act like it was anything but a good thing that I was pregnant. "I think it's the humidity and heat."

Miss Caroline gave me a wink. "I don't think so. What can I get you, you sweet young thing?" She was one to talk—for a woman in her fifties, she still looked fantastic. Maybe my momma was right about sea air and humidity being the key to keeping youthful looking skin. And Miss Caroline had a style to her. Her short brown hair with red highlights looked good no matter the weather, and her willowy figure was to be envied.

I bit my lip. "I'm waiting for somebody."

"It isn't my son by chance, is it?"

I shook my head. "I haven't seen Dallas since I got back into town. How is he?"

"Still single." Her smile held mischief.

"Miss Caroline."

"I can dream. You two were so cute together."

I didn't picture Dallas being too keen on dating me in my condition, and I was definitely not interested in him. He was the boy of every teenage girl's dream and he knew it. I doubt that attitude of his had changed. I rested my hand on my abdomen. "I already have a man."

"Sons are the best men to have."

I nodded in agreement.

"But someone to curl up with at night isn't a bad thing either."

She had me smiling. And so did the man that walked our way.

Miss Caroline turned to see who caught my attention. She looked between the two of us as Declan neared. "Looks like you already have someone in mind."

"We're friends," I got out before Declan could hear.

"You keep telling yourself that, honey. I'll be back to take your order. Declan." She gave him the once over as she walked away.

Declan tipped his head. "Miss Caroline." He dropped down next to me once she was out of sight. "Why do I get the feeling she doesn't like me?"

"Why wouldn't she?" I refused to divulge any of the conversation that had just taken place.

"Don't play coy, Miss Dixon, though it is becoming on you."

I gave him a little nudge. "Dallas and I are ancient history."

"Sometimes history repeats itself."

"That never turns out well."

His gaze intensified. "Are you sure?"

I bit my lip and nodded.

He pulled on a curl. "I won't argue with you, but sometimes it's not a bad thing to revisit the past."

"All I can focus on is the future."

His lips curled into a smile. "The future it is. Speaking of which, congratulations. Your dad told me the good news."

"When did you talk to him?"

"Yesterday. I met him on site. They broke ground on the Lawrence building."

"Oh, yeah. I guess I will need to know these things and get the lingo down."

"Just remember Redline. We're the best."

"We'll have to see about that. I'll be going over all our accounts and vendors." I teased him.

"I guess I know who to suck up to now."

"Is that what you call what you do?"

"It's a great sales tactic."

I laughed at him.

"At least I know I can still make you laugh." He always had a knack for it.

"Well, I'm starving and we have lots to do."

"Yes, ma'am." He picked up a menu on the coffee table in front of us.

I already knew what I was ordering. "Where do you want to focus today? I've mapped out Charleston and Indigo Bay based on the price range you gave me."

He kept his eyes on the menu. "What's your opinion? Where do you think you'll end up now that you're working for your dad?"

"All that counts is your opinion. It's your place."

"Of course your opinion matters, that's why I asked you to help me."

"They both have advantages, but honestly, the Charleston area is probably a better investment."

He set down his menu and turned so he was facing me. "You sound disappointed by that."

"It's silly, but there's this red bungalow near the pier that I've kind of fallen in love with, but it's more than I wanted to spend and it's impractical."

"Have you made an offer, tried to talk them down?"

"I haven't even gone to look at it because I'm afraid if I do I'll fall head over heels for it and it will cloud my judgment."

He pressed his lips together and thought for a moment. "That house is our first stop today."

"Declan, I'm trying to be sensible."

"What happened to the girl that was always first to go off

the high-dive or sneak out to swim in the ocean in the middle of the night with her boyfriend who shall go unnamed?"

I did my best not to smile or remember those hot summer nights I never wanted to end spent in his arms under a blanket of water. "She had to grow up."

His eyes roved over me from my head all the way down my long legs and back up until his eyes engaged mine. "I can see that she grew up, but when I look into her eyes, I see the fearless girl I once knew."

For an insane moment, I wanted to get lost in his eyes, in him. I wanted to pull him to me and do more than remember how it felt to be in his arms. I wanted to see if he still tasted like mint and honey. I needed and wanted to know if I was still desirable. But my son kicked and I remembered where my focus needed to be. And that I had been tossed aside. I couldn't be that fearless girl anymore. Too many of my fears had come true. I put some distance between us. "I think I'll stick to Charleston." That made the most sense.

His shoulders dropped. "Charleston it is."

⁓

We toured some new condos by the river, close to where he was already renting an apartment. Declan didn't seem all that impressed or interested. In each place we toured, I pulled out the drawing Halle had made me of the nursery. I tried to envision the dude ranch themed baby's room in each place, but I wasn't feeling it.

"I think I want a yard. I'm tired of living in apartments." Declan stated as we walked between units.

"Oh. You should have said something."

"I just did." He grinned.

"Well, there are a few historic homes for sale nearby, but they're pricey and you never know what you're getting into when you go that route. Or we could look more in the suburbs."

"How about we go look at that bungalow?"

"No."

"Come on. Maybe I want to buy it."

"It's way outside of your price range."

"I'm a good negotiator."

"I'll give you the address and you can go later."

"Mel, you know you want to."

"You sound like you're trying to dare me to sing karaoke with you."

He laughed. "We made a good Sonny and Cher."

"We were ridiculous and you sang off key."

"That's cold, Mel. And to make up for it, I insist we tour the house by the pier."

"Are those some of your sales tactics? Blackmail?"

"I like to think of it as a bribe."

I found myself smiling more when he was around. "That sounds so much better."

"How's this? We tour the house and I take you to dinner afterward."

"You already paid for my lunch."

"I didn't realize there was a daily limit."

I sighed. "I don't want the heartbreak of loving the house and not being able to have it."

He took my hand, making us both stand in place. "It's okay to dream."

"You don't know what I've been through."

"Tell me."

"Declan." I looked down at our clasped hands. Déjà vu ran through me and did it ever feel good. I pulled away.

He was reluctant to let go.

"We hardly know each other anymore."

"I want to change that." There was definite meaning behind those words and his smoldering look.

"You know all I have to offer is friendship, right?" I looked down at my growing midsection.

"I'll take whatever you can give me."

Why did I feel like I wanted to give him my heart?

Chapter Nine

∾

WE DIDN'T TOUR THE RED BUNGALOW. I DIDN'T HAVE IT IN me. I wasn't even sure why I was so obsessed with it. But every time I pulled it up on my tablet, it captivated me. I could see my little boy and me playing in the sand. And I'm sure his nursery would look perfect in the little red house.

Declan was also beginning to catch my attention. We ended up going through some model homes in a new subdivision just outside of Charleston. It touted a great school district and a family friendly community. Declan seemed more interested in the single-family homes than he had been in the condos. He was also interested in starting a family someday. As far as I could tell he was going to make a great husband and father.

I tried to remember if that's how I felt when I started seeing Greyson. I think I saw more of the business man. I admired him for his intelligence and drive. And his pursuit of me was breathtaking. I was a different person at twenty-five, with different priorities.

Now I watched a man think about if the backyard was big enough to build his future children a swing set. I never knew how attractive that could be.

I did my best not to think about Declan later that night as I looked over all the brochures I picked up from the home-builder in Charleston, but it was hard not to. Especially since Declan was trying to talk me into buying plots next to each other. He claimed I was the best neighbor he'd ever had. None of the homes spoke to me, though they were beautiful and in my price range. I loved the southern architecture and deep porches the homes offered, but the red bungalow reminded me of Nantucket and evoked feelings of home. But it was impractical and so expensive. Another thing not to think about.

There were some things—or should I say people—that were not letting me forget. I looked at my phone and a Facebook notification popped up. I hadn't had one in forever since I had sworn off social media while I was going through my divorce. The only thing I had done was change my name back to Melanie Dixon. That had garnered a lot of private messages from old friends. I stared at my phone. Declan had sent me a friend request. That was kind of cute, like him. Except he was more than cute.

I decided *what the heck* and logged in to Facebook to accept his friend request. And maybe I flipped through all the pictures he had posted over the last several years. There were quite a few of him at the Spartan Races he'd been talking so much about. Some of them looked professional, like the ones of him crawling under barbed wire and scaling huge walls. It got my blood pumping. There was this raw, sensual quality about him in the photos. It was probably a good thing I didn't take him up on his offer to watch him. I was already having a hard enough time resisting his charm and what I was sure were his subtle advances. But I did enjoy his company.

I scrolled through some more pictures. I loved his family

photos, especially the ones with his niece and nephew. There was a particularly sweet one where he was cradling his infant niece. The adoration on his handsome face was apparent. I had to quit looking. It was like the red bungalow—another disappointment in the making.

But I did decide that I was going to come out of the shell I had been in for the last several months. I felt like I had been hibernating. I posted one of the ultrasound pictures with the caption, *My son.* I also went through and deleted my wedding album and any other Greyson related pictures. I didn't even stop and pause to look at any of the old photos, what used to be some of my most treasured memories. I had wasted too many tears over the man.

While I was deleting photos, my feed blew up with comments. A ton of people were congratulating me. I was more than surprised to see that some of my "old friends" from Philadelphia were among them. Women I probably should have unfriended by the way they treated me when Greyson left me, but that wasn't my style. But it is one of the reasons I stayed off social media. I was hurt when pictures of parties and lunches that I would have normally been invited to popped up. I felt like the girl who sat alone at lunch.

More fun was in store. A new notification popped up that I had been tagged in a photo. I clicked on it and I couldn't believe what I saw. There I was standing out on one of the condo balconies Declan and I had looked at today. I was looking out over the river. My aviators were on, the light breeze ruffled through my hair and pink t-shirt dress. The way the sun fell on me gave the picture an artistic feel. He captioned the photo, *Beautiful Mel.*

If I thought the ultrasound picture was garnering its fair share of comments, it had nothing on this picture. We were going to be the talk of the town. Mutual friends from forever ago started commenting and asking if we were back together. I started receiving private messages asking if Declan was the father of my baby. People that I didn't know were commenting asking him the same question. He created a firestorm.

I texted him, *Did you see what you did? Please take that picture down.*

That will only look more suspicious.

You're enjoying this, aren't you?

Yes, ma'am.

I didn't give you permission to take that picture. I didn't even know that he had.

I couldn't help myself. Look how beautiful you are.

Flattery is not helping your case.

I'm being sincere.

That's not helping you either. Have you read the comments? They're great.

People are leaping to conclusions.

That's the fun part. It was like I could hear him laugh.

Goodnight.

Sweet dreams, Mel. Thanks for your help today.

I couldn't stay irritated with him. He was too sweet for my own good. *You're welcome.* Though I wasn't sure how much I'd helped him.

I looked at the photo one more time, doing my best not to read the comments. For a moment, I felt beautiful. I hadn't felt that way in too long. It was like I was seeing how Declan saw me. And that more than anything scared me.

I closed out the app only to see that Halle and Heather had sent me several text messages in our group chat we'd had forever, all in regards to the photo Declan posted.

OMG. OMG. That was Heather.

You look gorgeous. That was Halle.
Are you reading the comments?
He still has it bad for you.
What are you going to do?

I took a moment to breathe. *I'm going to leave well enough alone,* I texted back before putting my phone away. At least that was the plan. But my plans as of late didn't seem to be working out the way I thought.

I rubbed my baby. *It's you and me kid.*

My Sunday was a barrage of messages. I was tired of telling people that Declan and I were only friends. But I received one message I never expected from someone who I thought I would never see or hear from again. My ex-mother-in-law texted me. I didn't even know she knew how to text. All it said was, *I need to know the truth. Are you carrying my grandson?*

I sat stunned when I read it. I supposed she got wind of my Facebook post somehow. I thought about not responding. After all, she and her son both humiliated me with accusations. And she had turned her back on me. I had loved her like a mother and she discarded me. I simply texted back, *No.* I blocked and deleted her. I never wanted anything do with the Ellis' again. Legally and in all the ways that counted, this baby was mine and only mine; Greyson made sure of it.

I was so glad to see Monday come. I needed to work and get back into a routine.

I sat at the table in the kitchen with my parents before Daddy and I left for work. Daddy sipped on his coffee and read the paper. Momma was going over her schedule for the day. I enjoyed my yogurt parfait and read more comments on that post of Declan's. My favorite new one was from some guy named Jeff. *Dude, is your girlfriend pregnant?*

Declan's responses weren't making it clear enough that we weren't a couple. He was causing trouble.

Case in point. Momma looked up from her tablet. "I ran into Lucille Sanderson early this morning while Karen and I were walking. Lucille was out walking her dog."

I cringed. She was the biggest busybody. "Did her shoes match her dog's collar?"

Daddy snorted.

Momma's grin said they did. "She mentioned a face thingy post about you and Declan." Momma was obviously not social media savvy, but it didn't surprise me that Miss Lucille was. It was another avenue for her to glean gossip.

I placed my spoon in my parfait cup. Both my parents were now giving me their attention. "Declan posted a picture of me. No big deal."

"Lucille was under the impression you two were together and that the baby was his."

"Declan said no such thing."

"I suppose he also didn't say you were beautiful."

I decided I should get back to eating. Breakfast, after all, was the most important meal of the day.

Momma and Daddy laughed.

"That's what I thought," Momma wouldn't let it alone.

I swallowed and decided to change the subject. I needed to get their take on Tamara. I felt anxious about her contacting me. "Greyson's mom texted me last night."

Daddy dropped his paper and Momma's face turned a fiery shade of red.

"I know. I'm as surprised as you. She asked if the baby was Greyson's."

"How dare she," Momma lashed out.

Daddy took her hand to calm her.

"I told her no."

"Good for you, baby girl." Daddy kept a hold of Momma.

"Did she respond?" Momma was trying to temper her words.

"I don't know. I blocked her."

"You seem worried." Daddy was good at picking up on my mood.

"I thought I was done with their family. I want a clean break." Even though it had been nothing but messy. "And, honestly, her actions hurt me as much as Greyson's."

Momma was closest to me. She reached out and took my hand. "I never liked her. You are better off without the two of them."

I wasn't sure how true that was. The two women seemed to get along all right when things were good between my ex-husband and myself. But I do think Momma was a tad jealous at times since we lived in the same city as Tamara.

"I know, Momma." I squeezed her hand back. "I just don't want any interference after everything they put me through."

Daddy sat up straight, giving off the protector vibe. "She will have to get through me first. I should have hauled you home from the start." Oh, he had tried, but I resisted. I was going to make Greyson acknowledge this baby and restore my good name, but sometimes you have to know when to walk away.

"Thank you, Daddy. I'm sure it's nothing."

They both nodded, but unease hung in the air.

I tried to push it out of my mind as I started my first day at Dixon Construction. Daddy had my office next to his ready to go when I got there, complete with a dozen pink roses on my reclaimed wood desk. In the history of dads, he was the best. I focused on the finances first. I acquainted myself with the accounting software and dug right in to entering expenses and doing some comparisons of actual costs versus estimated. I felt like me. The numbers spoke to me. I needed this.

I was up and stretching my back around lunchtime when I had a visitor.

He peeked his head in my glass door. "Looks like you need a better chair. Or a massage. I can provide the latter."

I turned and flashed a quick smile at the man who kept popping up. "Here to start more rumors?"

He laughed and stepped in. "Sounds like fun, but no."

"Maybe for you."

"How about I make it up to you by buying you lunch to celebrate your first day? There's a cart vendor a few streets over that sells the most amazing soft pretzels. And I know how much you love those."

"What if I don't anymore?"

He slid close enough to wrap me up in his senses. "Then say the word and I'll take you anywhere you want to go."

My eyes drifted toward the closet in my office. I had the urge to drag him in there and see if he could still take my breath away. Instead I stepped away and took a deep breath. "Uh. I have a lot of work to do, and I packed a lunch."

He wasn't deterred. Desire filled his eyes. "Perfect. We'll walk to the park and eat there. I packed a lunch too."

"What are the odds of you taking no for an answer?"

"I'm not familiar with the word." That's what placed him on top of his career. And I knew it was an innocent statement. He never once took advantage of me. His blues peered into my own; they didn't beg, but they enticed. "You need the break and you know you want to. We can even hit the swings."

I stretched the twinge in my back. "Maybe a walk would do me some good."

A grin filled his face.

"Let me run to the restroom." Lately, I always had to run there first. I've never peed so much in my life.

"I'll say hi to your dad. Take your time."

All the way to the restroom and back I wondered what I was doing. I was smart enough to know that we were both attracted to each other, though I couldn't figure out why he was to me under the circumstances. But we hardly knew each other anymore, and well, I had no business entertaining anything more than friendship at this time in my life, maybe even for the rest of my life. But it was so easy to be around him. In some ways, it was like we were never apart.

I met Declan in Daddy's office. The two men were talking shop. Daddy loved nothing more. It sounded like he was trying to haggle a better price on equipment if we agreed to use Redline for an additional project.

"Let me see what I can come up with." Declan loved to play the game just as much. I could see the spark in his eye.

Daddy's eyes sparkled for me, though, when he was alerted to my presence. "There's the woman of the hour." Daddy met me by the door and kissed my cheek. "She's going to do great things here. And maybe you can talk Declan down."

"She may have some sway." Declan grinned.

I rolled my eyes at both of them. "Are you ready to go?" I held up my canvas lunch bag.

"Yes, ma'am." Declan shook hands with Daddy. "See you later, Mr. Dixon."

"You can call me Rich." Daddy gave him a hearty pat on the back.

Declan seemed touched. "Thank you, sir."

"Have a good lunch, you two." Daddy gave me an impish smile.

It wasn't going to be that good. Even if part of me wanted it to be.

Declan grabbed his lunchbox from the Redline company truck. It looked like all the trucks in that industry, big and white with their logo plastered on the door and tailgate. He looked good with the sun shining on his sandy brown hair. His skin already looked kissed by the sun. I think he ran outdoors a lot training for his Spartan Races. Along with a lot of weight training and doing odd things like tossing spears. It was apparently intense.

His smiled warmed me more than the sun as he neared, and we headed to the park two blocks away. It felt good to be out. I loved this time of year in South Carolina, not too hot or humid yet.

We walked close together; our arms touched more than once.

"You know, Miss Lucille is now spreading rumors that you are the father of my baby."

He laughed. "I can think of worse things to be accused of."

"You're a troublemaker."

"You used to be one, too."

"Not really."

"Who took her parents' car while they were out of town and drove us all to Greenville to see The Killers in concert?"

"We didn't get caught, so that doesn't count."

"Does your tattoo count?"

I faced forward and tried not to smile. I thought about that day, Declan's eighteenth birthday. He wanted to get a tattoo, I guess as a christening into adulthood. I went with him and something came over me. I wanted one too. I totally begged the tattoo artist to do it. I wasn't legal yet, and there was no way my parents were going to give me permission. I talked him into doing a small red heart at the small of my back. I hid it from my parents for several weeks, but I got careless when summer rolled around—my bikini bottoms didn't cover it. They were furious at me and even Declan. I had to stop them from turning in the tattoo parlor to the state board. I was grounded for two weeks. I still snuck out to see the man who now walked next to me.

"Do you still have it?" His voice was so enticing.

I gave a small nod. "Do you still have yours?"

He rolled up his sleeve. *Mel* was scrolled across his muscular upper arm.

I stopped and stared at it. When I was seventeen I thought that was the most romantic thing ever. I wanted to run my fingers over it, but I couldn't. "I'm sorry you permanently marked yourself with my name. I bet the women in your life have hated it."

"I would do it all over again." He rolled down his sleeve. "And I've only had one serious complaint."

I felt myself blush. I began our walk again toward the park.

"I was engaged." He answered the question on my mind.

I wasn't shocked by the news. I was more surprised he wasn't married. "I'm sorry you broke up. Or did you?" I grinned.

"It's been a while. I'm over it."

"I hope you didn't break up over the tattoo."

"If we did, I would say that was a good indicator we shouldn't have gotten married. But, yeah, she wasn't fond of it."

"Maybe you'll find a Melody or Melania."

"Or a Melanie."

Or one of those.

Chapter Ten

○✺○

I FOUND MYSELF GOING TO LUNCH WITH DECLAN OFTEN over the next couple of weeks. I was seeing him more than Halle and Heather. Heather had moved on from my doctor, thank goodness. He admitted that he was a huge *Star Trek* fan and went to Comic Cons, and that was a total turn off for her. All wasn't lost though, she moved on to his colleague Dr. Martin. They met during a date—Heather had been with Dr. Winters, and Dr. Martin was with another woman. Leave it to Heather to pick up a man when she's out with another man. But not only was Heather occupied with the new doctor, Halle was suddenly busy all the time, and happy, like downright giddy. Her excuse was some new herbal treatment she was trying. I would have asked for some too if I wasn't pregnant and paranoid about everything that went into my body.

Sometimes during lunch, Declan and I would look at homes in the nearby area. Declan seemed really interested in the new subdivision we looked at the first round of house hunting. I just couldn't find anything that spoke to me or a place I could visualize the nursery. Declan kept trying to get me to make an appointment to see the red bungalow, but I couldn't. I knew my budget and I was sticking to it. I only needed to look harder for the right place. It would probably help if I didn't keep checking to see if the place by the pier had sold every day.

My parents were hoping I would wait until after the baby was born, and I was beginning to think they were right. By the time I negotiated, closed, and moved in, I would probably be right at my due date. It was frustrating. I always imagined when I was pregnant I would be decorating a nursery and nesting the whole time. I never pictured the craziness I'd been through.

I finally signed up for prenatal and breastfeeding classes. Those started in a week. I got my birth plan filled out. I was really hoping to go natural. I happened to watch a video of an epidural and no thank you. That needle was ridiculously long. The only question was who was going to be with me in the delivery room. My parents were out. I wasn't sure how Heather would handle it, and she might just push me to get drugs. But Halle would completely fight against any pain meds even if it was in my best interest to get them. Maybe if both came they would even each other out. I could always hire a doula.

More decisions to make.

My twenty-eight-week appointment came. I wasn't looking forward to taking the glucose test, but I had to admit I was looking forward to after the appointment. I had agreed to have lunch with Declan. He passed along to me from his sister to make sure I didn't eat anything sugary the day before the appointment and to be well hydrated. It was sweet he was giving me tips and that he was taking such an interest in my pregnancy. He seemed fascinated with it. He was even good enough to bring me a lumbar seat for my office chair.

He was the best friend ever. I was doing my best to keep it on the friendly side and he was good at reading me, so he wasn't pushing it further. That was good, because I think he would be hard to resist.

It was another beautiful day, so I decided to walk to my appointment. It only took fifteen minutes. I signed in and did all the fun stuff like pee in a cup and get weighed. I had gained three pounds, which was a good thing. Then the torture began. They gave me this awful drink that tasted like concentrated orange soda. I barely got it down it was so disgusting. I gagged on it and felt like I was going to vomit. The nurse informed me if I did I would have to retake it. I really wanted to know who came up with these torturous events. I had to suffer for an hour, sitting there willing myself not to lose the contents of my stomach. It was uncomfortable too, as I had to stay in the waiting area. I'm sure I looked ridiculous doing whatever I could to keep my mind off how nauseated I felt. Anything from walking around to shifting every which way in my chair. And I was taking deep breaths like I was in labor.

I made it through the hour. That's when the real fun began. Normally, blood doesn't make me queasy at all, but I was in no state of mind when they drew my blood to test for the glucose levels. I lost it as soon as the nurse pulled the needle out. Yep, right there in the wastebasket. I've rarely been so embarrassed. To make matters worse I kept vomiting and then dry heaving. I had nurses running around all over trying to help me. Dr. Winters even got into the fray. The pretty-boy doctor finally set me up in an exam room. They got me comfortable on a table, threw a blanket over me, and turned down the lights, only keeping the ones that were above the counters on.

I was mortified as I lay there in the fetal position. I completely forgot about my lunch date until my phone buzzed about a hundred times. At a snail's pace, I moved to reach into my purse that the nurses set on the chair next to me.

Declan had tried to call numerous times. I felt even worse. We had planned to meet at the new deli near the medical district. Even thinking about food made me want to throw up some more, even though there wasn't anything left to go except the sips of water I had taken.

I called him and he immediately answered. "Are you okay?" Panic ran through every word.

"Yes and no." I related my embarrassing tale.

"I'm coming to get you."

"You don't have to do that. I'll call my dad or maybe I'll feel better and I can walk back."

"Give me the address. I'll be in there five minutes."

"I don't want you to see me like this."

"Mel, I held your hair when you puked your guts out after drinking tequila for the first time."

I had forgotten all the stupid and illegal stuff I had done with him around. "Okay." I gave him the address and went back to ruing my existence. This was worse than all the morning sickness I'd ever had. That glucose should come with a warning label.

As promised, he was there in minutes. A nurse saw him back. He moved my purse and took the seat next to me. He stroked my head and hair. "I'm sorry you don't feel good."

I opened my eyes to see the care and concern in his. His face was closer than I thought it would be. It was kind of nice.

"Why didn't you bring anyone with you?"

Tears welled up in my eyes. "I didn't know I would need to. Besides, I have to do this alone."

He caressed my cheek, wiping tears as they fell. "Why?"

"Because the one person that should have been here cheated on me and left me when I told him I was pregnant. He hated the thought of my baby so much he legally signed away any rights to him. Not only that, he told everyone the baby wasn't his. I can't count on anyone." I don't know why I was telling Declan all these things. Maybe so he would know where my head was or how broken I felt. The tears streamed down my face.

Even in the low light I saw Declan's face tighten and change colors to a deep shade of red. "There are no words for what a piece of garbage he is."

"You left me and accused me too." Now I really didn't know what I was saying. It was so long ago. But why did I still feel the sting of it? With perfect clarity, I could see him throw the promise ring into the ocean. I had never seen him behave in such a way. I curled more into myself. I felt so stupid bearing my soul to him like this.

His blue eyes widened, but his whole upper body seemed to deflate as he let out a huge breath. His hand rested on my cheek. "You don't know how much I've regretted that over the years."

"It doesn't matter. I shouldn't have said anything."

"It does matter, Mel. You matter. Your baby matters. I'm so sorry I ever hurt you."

I closed my eyes. The emotions I felt coursing between us were too much at the moment. "I don't feel good."

"Rest." He kissed my forehead. "I'm not going anywhere." His tenderness only kept the tears flowing.

I wasn't sure how long I lay there with Declan stroking my hair and rubbing my arm, but the nausea began to subside about the time Dr. Winters came in to check on me. He brought with him water, crackers, and his shiny smile.

I slowly sat up and ran my fingers through my curls. I no doubt looked like a train wreck.

Dr. Dreamy didn't seem as interested with my new guest as he was with the ones I brought last time. Probably because Declan was better looking than him, at least I thought so. But he did shake his hand and introduce himself. I hoped he wasn't going to mention Heather. And thankfully he never did.

I would have probably gotten a new doctor if it wasn't for the fact I was already so far along, and I'd had enough disruptions in my care. I took a few sips of the water and rested the package of crackers in my lap. I was wary of any food.

Dr. Winters gave me a quick look over. "Why don't you come back tomorrow for your appointment? I'll have the front desk work you in."

I nodded, grateful. I wanted nothing more than to get out of there.

Dr. Winters helped me off the table. From there Declan wrapped his arm around me. "Let's get you home."

I leaned into him and took comfort in his familiar embrace. But there was more to it. Something that felt new. He was no longer the boy who had captured my heart. It was as if I was incredibly aware of the man and what his hold was telling me. For the first time in months I felt wanted, but that terrified me.

Declan talked me into going home instead of to the office. It's not like Daddy minded, but I didn't want anyone to think I was getting special treatment. But all I wanted was my bed and to pretend my little episode never happened.

"Your doctor is sure pretty." I guess that was Declan's attempt to make small talk while he drove me home.

I rolled my head toward him and smiled. "Not as pretty as you."

"Miss Dixon, are you complimenting me?" I loved when he pretended to be Southern.

"Thank you."

He reached over and brushed his hand over my hair as if to say it was his pleasure helping me, but his grin took a lighter turn. "I want you to do something for me."

"What?"

"I want you to come watch me race this weekend."

"In North Carolina?"

"It's only a three-hour drive."

'I'm pregnant, so add an hour to that time." Three hours meant two to three restroom breaks.

"Does that mean you'll come?"

"I don't know."

"I'll map out the cleanest bathrooms and bring your favorite snacks."

"Declan."

"Please, Mel. I really want to share this with you." He knew how to get to me.

I took a deep breath and let it out. "The snacks better be really good."

His laughter filled the cab of his truck.

I missed that sound. I was realizing how much I missed him. I wasn't sure how to process that. I hadn't been pining over him, but now that he was back in my life he seemed to fill a piece of me that I hadn't realized was missing. What did that mean?

Chapter Eleven

DECLAN'S START TIME WAS 10:00 A.M., WHICH MEANT WE had to leave at five in the morning. Even the baby protested by kicking when my alarm went off at 4:00 a.m. I was right there with him. We needed a few more hours of sleep on a Saturday. My body was exhausted from growing a human, starting a new job, trying to figure out my life, shooting down the rumors about Declan and me, house hunting, and last but certainly not least, keeping Declan at arm's length. That last one was maybe the toughest of them all. He was doing his best to make his intentions known, all while not pushing it. I'm telling you, he was a good salesman.

I rubbed my little guy when I crawled out of bed. I was officially twenty-nine weeks today. Dr. Winters said everything looked good and his office called yesterday to say I didn't have gestational diabetes. Thank goodness. That one test had me rethinking having more than one child. And I was never ever going near orange soda again.

My appointments were now every two weeks until I hit thirty-six weeks and then they would be weekly until this little man made his appearance. I was still grappling with his name. I didn't want anything trendy or dated, but I wanted it to be strong, to give him something to live up to.

Today the weather was supposed to be warm, but with a chance of rain. I had a built-in heater, so after I showered I threw on some white shorts, I would say cute, but we are talking maternity clothes. The off-the-shoulder trumpet sleeved blouse added some style. Momma had bought it for me when she was out and about a few days ago. She had excellent taste and I loved that she was so thoughtful. Or maybe she was telling me I needed to look nice for Declan. Either way, I hoped I was as good of a momma as her.

I looked in the mirror. The blush blouse looked good against my creamy skin. I looked more pregnant than I had the day before. I let my curls fall naturally. Straightening them in the humidity was pointless. I slipped into some leather wedges and grabbed my bag that I packed the night before with essentials like sunscreen and lip gloss.

Declan said he was handling all the food. He was so excited I was coming. I had almost forgotten what it was like to have a man desire my company.

Declan rapped lightly on the front door. I'm sure my parents appreciated not being woken up.

I opened the door with my bag slung around my shoulder ready to go. I stood still to take him in. He looked like he had gone rogue, and it suited him. He hadn't shaved in a couple of days and his athletic clothing showed every line and muscle he had. If he was trying to sell me on the package, I was ready to sign on the dotted line. I let out a deep breath. "Wow."

He flexed his biceps. "Impressive, huh?"

"I don't remember you being so full of yourself."

"You need to remember harder. You ready to go?"

I nodded and followed him out, locking the door behind me.

He held my hand on the way to his truck.

I looked down at our joined hands and then back up to meet his hungry eyes.

"I'm done being subtle." His grip firmed up.

I was afraid of that. "Declan…"

"I know, Mel."

"Do you?"

"I know you're scared and I understand, but all I'm asking for is a chance."

"What if I'm not ready to make that decision?"

He pulled my hand up and his warm lips fell upon it. "I'll wait for as long as it takes."

"I'm pregnant." That was such a dumb thing to say.

His smile said he agreed. "And you've never looked more beautiful. I know this is a package deal."

I bit my lip.

He brushed his thumb across my lips. "I love when you do that. I'm not asking you to make a decision today, or even tomorrow, or the next day. I'm just letting you know where I'm at."

I swallowed hard. "Okay."

He pulled me along. "Let's go have some fun." He certainly knew how to start the day off with a bang.

My heart was beating like I had run a race. It didn't settle down until we were outside Indigo Bay's city limits. I kept my focus outside the truck. He had vaulted us into new territory.

"You aren't going to be shy around me now, are you?"

I turned from the window and faced him. "When have I ever been?"

He placed a hand on my bare knee. "Never." He was quick to remove it. "You're going to make me lose my racing edge."

"Hey, you invited me."

"I can't wait to cross the finish line and have you there."

I hesitated to ask, but I had been curious since he mentioned it. "Did you ever take your fiancée to these Spartan thingies?"

He chuckled. "First of all, these aren't thingies, this is serious stuff. And I met Maren at one; she raced too."

"Oh. Was she really into it the way you are?"

He nodded.

"Does this make you uncomfortable?"

A smile played on his lips. "No. I just wasn't expecting to talk about her with you."

"How long ago did you breakup?"

"You want the whole story?"

"How about a brief overview?" I wasn't sure I wanted to hear about the woman he almost married.

"We met three years ago, but didn't really start dating until a year after that. A year later we were engaged and we broke up right before the wedding six months later."

"It wasn't really that long ago then."

"Not long enough."

"Why did you break up?"

"Besides her being more jealous than I cared for, I can't really put my finger on it. But I knew it wasn't right. I think she knew too. After we broke up I started applying for positions out of state. I knew I needed to make a change. When this job came open here I jumped on it. And when I found out you were back I felt like life was giving me a second chance to undo the biggest mistake of my life."

"Declan, I don't know if you can make the biggest mistake of your life when you're eighteen."

"Being with you after all this time proves to me it was.

I've never met your equal. I've never felt for another woman the way I feel for you."

"I thought you were giving me time."

"I am. I just want you to know this isn't some adolescent crush."

I was trying to take in everything he was saying, but I needed more time to think. "We should probably change the subject."

He gave me a pressed smile before flipping on the radio. "All right, baby, let's jam."

Big fat smiles erupted. He always knew how to ease a situation. I hadn't had this much fun in forever. And I loved that I could be me. We rocked out in the car all the way to Charlotte—in between bathroom breaks and eating, my two favorite pastimes as of late. Declan had made some super yummy protein and healthy carb-packed breakfast sandwiches. He also still sang out of tune, but I didn't mind. Laughter and music filled the car as we sang over one another and forgot the lyrics.

It was perfect until we made it to our destination and I realized I should have asked Declan more about what I agreed to, or maybe he could have given me a better heads up. First of all, it was massive. The line of cars to the event took forever to get through. It was on a military installation out in the middle of nowhere. We had to park in a large field, which was fine, but it had started to rain.

"Um." I looked out of the truck, worried. "If it keeps raining, we're going to get stuck."

"I have four-wheel drive, and my weather app is saying the rain is moving off to the east."

I looked down at my shoes and outfit. "I think I overdressed."

"I think you look perfect."

I looked out at all the participants and spectators getting out of their vehicles and heading toward the event. They were all dressed in athletic clothes and wearing proper shoes for walking in fields and on muddy roads. "How can you say that? I look like one of those fussy Southern women who is afraid of getting dirty. You should have told me what I was signing up for. I thought there would be stands for spectators. Are there even bathrooms here?"

He slid across the bench seat with a sheepish grin. "How do you feel about porta-potties?"

"Please tell me you're joking."

His grin widened.

I scowled at him.

"I haven't seen that look in a long time."

"Expect that and more depending on how many times I have to use a porta-potty. Why didn't you tell me?"

"Honestly, I didn't think about it."

I sighed. "I'm going to look ridiculous."

"Impossible."

"You're just saying that."

He leaned in as if he was going to kiss me.

I held my breath, not sure how I felt about it. Of course I wanted him to, but I wasn't sure I was ready. I think he sensed my hesitation. He lingered inches away. "You don't know how much it means to me that you're here. I promise you, after this I'm going to take you to a nice fussy place for lunch with the cleanest bathrooms you've ever seen."

My lips betrayed me and smiled.

He moved back to his side of the truck. "You're definitely not helping my edge when you smile at me like that."

"Just promise me you'll run fast or do whatever it is you do."

"Deal." He opened his door and grabbed his bag.

I hesitated. I wasn't a prissy woman, but I wasn't looking forward to muddy feet or porta-potties. But for Declan I would deal with it.

He met me on my side and helped me out of the truck. The ground covered in massive weeds wasn't too muddy yet. But I wobbled on the uneven ground in my wedges. Declan took my hand and steadied me.

I kept shaking my head wishing I would have worn tennis shoes. I had an umbrella, but no one else was using one and I didn't want to look more out of place. "You so owe me."

He laughed and kissed my wet head.

Once we hit the gravel road that led to registration and the entrance it was better, but it didn't help how different I looked compared to everyone else.

There were throngs of people coming and going. Races started every half hour, so there were men and women that had finished and were already leaving. Some of them looked beyond exhausted, but many looked elated. Pride beamed out of their eyes. I guessed it was quite the accomplishment. They were all wearing the same shirt that read "Finisher" on the back.

I stayed behind and did some more people watching while Declan got his registration packet. Loud music played and there were several vendor booths selling all sorts of athletic gear and food. There were even little children. It looked like they held a mini event for kids. I wondered if my little guy would ever want to. I imagined he would if Declan was in our lives. That was a weird thought. Not at all unpleasant, but dangerous. I couldn't bear another broken heart, and now it wasn't only my heart on the line. I placed my hand on my moving belly. My son was my first thought and consideration.

Declan walked back to me all smiles with his Spartan headband on. Every racer wore them along with a plastic tracking bracelet. He also had some company with him. Leave it to Declan to make friends at the registration table. A woman and a teenage boy. The boy must be racing as he was also wearing a headband, but the woman looked wary. I'm guessing she was his mother.

"Mel, this is Jill and Kyle."

I held out my hand to shake Jill's and then Kyle's hand. "It's nice to meet you."

Declan patted Kyle on the back. "This is his first time."

Jill gave a weak smile. She looked too young to have a teenage son. "My husband was supposed to run with him, but he was deployed last month."

"That must be terribly difficult."

"It never gets easier. Kyle wanted to race anyway to honor his dad."

I had so much respect for military families. "I'm sure he loves that."

Gangly thin and tall, Kyle shrugged like it was no big deal.

"I'm not really sure about him running and I just signed a waiver that warned of the possibility of him dying."

I met Declan's eyes. "Is that true?"

Declan gave me and Jill his best salesman smile. "No one is going to die. Their lawyers make them put that in there."

I don't think that made Jill feel better. I know I didn't.

Declan faced Jill. "I'll keep Kyle under my wing the whole time. We'll jump over the fiery finish line together."

My eyebrows hit my bangs. "You have to jump over fire?"

Declan wagged his eyebrows. "That's the fun part."

Kyle's brown eyes lit up while his mom's brow furrowed.

Jill pulled her son to her for a long hug. Kyle looked embarrassed but he was smart enough not to pull away.

Declan took me in his arms. "You used to kiss me for luck before a race," he whispered in my ear.

We locked eyes and was I ever tempted, but my lips landed on his unshaven cheek. "That's for the porta-potty."

He laughed but pulled me closer. "I'm giving you fair warning. I'm going to own your lips when I cross that finish line."

I shivered in the drizzly rain. "You're not playing fair."

"I'm not playing." He kissed my cheek before releasing me. He handed me his bag to keep while he raced. It held the clothes he would change into afterward.

I had to catch my breath. I watched him and Kyle walk off together with lots of emotions coursing through me. Everything from worry to anticipation. I didn't expect him back in my life, and now I wasn't sure what to do.

Jill joined my side. "We can watch them take off. And I have a map of the course, so we can catch some of the obstacles."

I nodded still trying to gather my thoughts.

"Your husband is so sweet—

"Um ... Declan's not my husband."

Her cheeks tinted red. "I'm so sorry, I just assumed." She looked at my belly. "Never mind."

I smiled at her. "I'm pregnant."

She let out a sigh of relief. "I should know better to assume such things."

"Really, it's okay. It's complicated. I'm divorced and Declan is ... I'm not sure."

She smiled. "I've been in your shoes." She looked down at my ridiculous out-of-place leather wedges. That were probably ruined. "Well, maybe not your exact shoes."

"Ugh. Declan didn't give me any warning about what I was in for today."

She laughed. "Well, at least Tanner, my husband, was good enough to do that."

"That's a good man."

She pointed at Declan and Kyle at the starting line with a hundred or so other crazy people. Declan looked like he was giving Kyle a pep talk. "Looks like you have a good man too."

"He is." I watched him animatedly talk to Kyle while stretching and jumping up and down trying to keep his muscles loose. His fantastic muscles that felt perfect around me.

"You don't sound sure."

"I'm not sure about us."

She went to respond, but the announcer got on his bull horn. It was time for the race to start. Declan caught my eye one last time. I mouthed good luck. He gave me a wink.

Poor Jill looked beside herself. "I can't believe I'm letting my fifteen-year-old do this."

"Declan won't let anything happen to him." I tried to give her some reassurance, but yeah, I didn't think I would be too keen on letting my son run a race where there was a risk of death and/or dismemberment.

Energy buzzed in the air right before they took off. All the participants shouted, "I am Spartan." And the gates opened. The participants spilled over the starting line. There were teams dressed all the same, pairs, and individuals of all ages and from all walks of life. It was an inspiring sight. It didn't make me want to do one, but the vibe was intoxicating.

Jill was good enough to show me where the porta-potties were before we headed to the first obstacles we could watch, the ropes and the rings. I was cursing Declan as I trudged through the mud in the most inappropriate shoes, to pee in what was the most disgusting place ever. It didn't help that I was seven months pregnant.

I was determined to wait if I had to use the restroom again until we had lunch. But how was I going to go anywhere with filthy shoes and feet and looking like a drowned rat? Maybe we could stop for some wipes. But I had bigger things to worry about, like Declan kissing me. Allowing him to kiss me was like an unofficial commitment. Or was it a commitment? He already stated his intention that he was looking for a relationship. Sure, he said he would be patient and I believed him, but kissing was serious business. It said something, at least for me.

Jill was giving me a sympathetic smile as I walked toward her. The rain had picked up. I finally saw some spectators with umbrellas. I was already wet, but still pulled mine out.

"You look too pretty to be here." She stared at my white shorts.

"He owes me big time."

"I have a feeling he won't mind paying up."

I had the same feeling. It thrilled and frightened me.

At least some of the paths were paved. They wound around old barracks and what looked like abandoned buildings. My guess was they played war games out here. That was a chilling thought.

We had some time to kill before any participants made it to these particular obstacles. According to the map, they had to face some challenging ones before even getting this far. There was some huge wall to climb that dropped off into muddy water. The barbed wire crawl also had to be completed. Declan said he could do this course in an hour or less. I was holding him to it. The rain wasn't letting up and I knew my bladder wouldn't wait forever.

"Where is your husband?" I asked Jill.

"Afghanistan. It's only a six-month deployment, but it was unexpected."

"I can't even imagine how tough that is."

"It's hardest on the kids."

"Kyle has siblings?"

She pulled out her phone under the protection of my umbrella and showed me her beautiful family. She had three kids, two boys and a girl.

"Kyle looks like your husband."

She laughed. "You think so?"

I tilted my head, not sure why she found humor in that.

"Tanner isn't his biological dad."

"Oh. I would have never guessed."

"No one does. Tanner is his father in all the ways that count. We married when Kyle was only two. Tanner is all Kyle has ever known."

"You're lucky." I kept a watch out for Declan and Kyle.

"You're worried about how Declan will feel about your baby?" She had great intuition.

"Yes. Among other things."

"Like I said, I've been there. I worried that Tanner didn't know what he was really getting into. And what was going to happen when we had children together? Would he love Kyle less?"

I leaned in more, anxious to hear her response.

She smiled at my eagerness. "If anything, I think he loved him more. Biology has very little to do with love. And DNA certainly doesn't make a father."

"That I know." I rested my hand on my abdomen. "But it's a little more complicated. This isn't Declan's and my first go around."

She raised her eyebrow. "If he's the right one then it doesn't matter how many laps you have to take to get there."

That was something to think about.

Chapter Twelve

DECLAN HAD NEVER BEEN MORE ATTRACTIVE TO ME AS I watched him help Kyle every step of the way. Even if it meant he wasn't finishing as quickly as my bladder and my muddy, wet feet had hoped. My admiration for him grew as I witnessed him encouraging Kyle to make it to the top of the rope climb, or how he painstakingly inched along with him on the rings even though I knew he could have zipped through them. But I was almost in tears when I watched him go back for a struggling Kyle carrying a huge sandbag up several flights of stairs. When they emerged together, Declan was bearing the weight of both sandbags.

Jill grabbed my hand with tears in her eyes. "Hold on to that one."

Oh, how I wanted to, but my heart wasn't so sure if it could handle another heartbreak.

The last obstacle we could see before we headed toward the finish line to wait was the javelin throw. Declan's first toss was on point. It took Kyle a few tries, but with Declan's coaching he completed the task.

Jill and I waited patiently, or not so patiently, for our guys to come around the last bend. We watched several participants finish the final obstacle, which was the herculean pull. It seemed cruel after everything else they had to do that at the finale they had to hoist a massive weight up a few stories. And then in their weakened state they had to jump over a line of fire. That made me nervous. I knew Jill was. She was so nervous she was gripping my arm, and I was a virtual stranger to her. But I felt like we had a kinship despite our very short acquaintance.

The rain was still coming down, but somehow the line of fire blazed. We were standing close enough to it to feel some heat from it. I couldn't believe Declan was going to be jumping over that any moment and that after almost twelve years he was going to kiss me. I popped a breath mint in my mouth to prepare physically. Emotionally there wasn't any preparation I could do. I knew this was a game changing moment. My heart felt like it had run the race.

Then Declan and Kyle appeared and my heart picked up the pace like it was going for a first-place win. I reached for my phone and took some more pictures of Declan and Kyle. Thankfully the case was waterproof. Kyle looked so relieved to see the end was near. Declan looked alive and sexier than I had ever seen him, even though he was filthy from head to toe. His sheer prowess was overwhelming. What was I getting myself into?

Declan's eyes caught mine for a brief second before he helped Kyle hoist his weight. His eyes were telling me to get ready. I gulped down a huge amount of nerves. I wasn't sure I had ever been this nervous or excited by a kiss.

Once Declan hoisted his own weight, he and Kyle sprinted toward the fire. Jill and I moved to stand on the other side of it. I put away my umbrella and captured as many photos as I could of Declan jumping over the blaze with command. Such satisfaction filled his features. He high-fived Kyle before he set his sights on me. I stood just feet away from him.

I had just enough time to shove my phone in my bag before he was running to me and picking me up. I didn't know how he had the strength to hold me up. He lifted me high enough, but with enough care of the belly that came between us, that my face looked down at his mud streaked one. I ran my hands across his handsome face and through his drenched hair. My hands knew him, my body knew him. A rush of emotion hit me and showed up in the form of tears. His eyes spoke of knowing me.

There in the noisy crowd, unspoken thoughts were said as the rain trickled down every inch of our skin and clung to our clothes, leaving no mystery to the shape beneath them. Our silent communication spoke of loss, regret, but mostly desire. Declan lowered me until all he had to do was lean in and capture my lips. He did so with a passion I had never felt. His lips, though the same, spoke differently than they used to. He was no longer a boy who at times felt unsure. This man knew exactly what he wanted. His pressing mouth compelled mine to part. I heard a small moan of pleasure as his lips consumed my very being. For a moment, I forgot that there was ever anybody but him. No man had ever touched me in such a way, not even him.

His brief kiss filled me up. And as soon as his lips danced off mine it was like the play button was clicked and the world around us started up again.

"Congratulations," I whispered, still in his arms.

He brushed my lips. "Thank you." He gently set me down, but took my hand.

We walked together to receive his medal for finishing and his "Finisher" t-shirt. Kyle and Jill were there. Both gave us sly grins. I'm sure we made a spectacle of ourselves, but we weren't the only ones giving congratulatory kisses. Though ours had very little to do with the race.

Kyle and Declan proudly wore their medals. I took pictures of them together. Jill gave me her number so I could text them to her and so we could keep in touch. I was happy to have had her company during the two-hour event. Jill couldn't wait to send them to her husband.

Jill hugged Declan and thanked him for taking such good care of her son. It was raining so hard now that Jill and Kyle just left. Declan wanted to change out of his filthy clothes first. I wished I had some dry clothes to change into.

Declan must have read my mind. He kissed the side of my head. "I have an extra shirt you can change into, though I do appreciate Mother Nature giving me a taste of your figure."

I smacked his arm. "Hit the changing tent."

He left, and I had to use the porta-potty one more time, unfortunately. My body refused to wait. I felt like I was entering a petri dish full of germs. I prayed nothing grew on me or in me. It was a good thing I was in such a euphoric state after that kiss or I may have had some violent thoughts over how uncomfortable and dirty I was. Hugging Declan all but ruined my pretty white shorts and blush blouse. And my leather wedges were never recovering. I didn't even want to see the state of my hair. Ha. The rain was moving off to the east my foot.

My next worry was how we were going to get out of the field the truck was parked in. It wasn't a pretty site when Declan and I arrived to what looked like a monster truck rally, except it was filled with sedans spinning their wheels doing their best to get out and onto the road. There were some good Samaritans trying to push people out, but only some were successful.

I bit my lip and looked down at my muddy feet, not sure how I was even going to walk to the truck.

Declan smiled at the mud bath before us and then down at my inadequate footwear. With no warning at all he scooped me up and off my feet. "Miss Dixon, I think I owe you a new pair of shoes."

I wrapped my arms around his neck. "You owe me a lot more than that. If I ever see a porta potty again it will be too soon."

He planted a quick kiss on my lips with a wicked grin. "You name it and it's yours."

"Anything?"

"I'm at your command."

"I like the sound of that. I'll start of easy. I'd like to be dry and I'm starving."

"I can fix that." He held me tight against him. He managed to carefully walk us to the truck without slipping.

When he set me in his truck it felt like the baby kicked my ribs. "Ow." I held my midsection.

"Are you okay?" Declan looked over every inch of me as if assessing me.

"I'm fine, it's just the baby reminding me he's here."

Declan leaned more into the truck trying to keep the moisture off him. "May I?"

I knew what he was asking and I nodded.

I thought he would rest his hand on top of my shirt, but instead he slid it under my shirt. It felt warm and perfect against my damp skin. His touch had me catching my breath. I moved his hand to where he could feel my son. I rested my hand on his. There I watched his eyes fill with wonder as the baby kicked. It was a beautiful moment.

"I can't wait to meet him."

Those were the sweetest words ever spoken to me. I leaned in and kissed him. I could taste my tears mixed in with the mint gum he had just chewed as our lips got tangled up. His tongue urged my lips apart. He deepened the kiss, sending my heart rate into a frenzy. The baby got excited too.

Declan felt him and smiled against my lips. "I think your son approves."

"You think so?"

"The only question now is, what does his mother think?"

Chapter Thirteen

WHAT DID THE MOTHER THINK?

It was so easy to think how wonderful life would be with him while I was wrapped up in his arms, swinging on the hammock, enjoying a lazy Sunday afternoon under the Carolina sun. He was obviously exhausted from his race the day before and slept soundly to the sound of the waterfall in my parents' pool. I was curled up next to him listening to the steady beat of his heart, drifting in and out of sleep myself. It was the picture of serenity, except my mind and even my heart wondered what I was doing.

Declan wasn't part of my plans when I moved home. I meant to stay away from the opposite sex unless I was related to them by blood. But being in Declan's arms felt so good and even right. Like I had finally made it home after a long absence.

Declan woke up, at least enough to kiss the top of my head and pull me tighter against him.

"Hey, troublemaker."

A sleepy laugh escaped him.

"I think we may need to take down your Facebook account."

"Not a chance. Where else would I post pictures of my beautiful girlfriend?"

"I'm your girlfriend now?"

"You were wearing my t-shirt yesterday."

"And thanks for posting that picture of me in it. What was your caption? She looks hot in my t-shirt."

"Well, you did."

"You know what people are going to think."

"That I'm a gentleman for lending you some dry clothes?"

"Nice try."

He shifted so our eyes could meet. "I would say I'm sorry, but I'm not."

"What am I going to do with you?"

He leaned in and pressed his warm lips against mine. His hands got tangled up in my hair. He tasted like citrus, sweet and tart. His kiss was long and slow like a waltz. We danced perfectly together like seasoned partners. I sighed and he groaned. It was the kind of kiss that could have gone on endlessly, but we had company.

Daddy cleared his throat.

I really needed to get my own place.

Declan and I broke apart only to grin at each other. Had this been twelve years ago, Declan would have jumped off the hammock and acted like it never happened. Now we lazily sat up together to face my smiling parents.

"Thought we could barbecue." Daddy grinned.

"I'll help." Declan jumped up. So maybe he did still feel intimidated by Daddy.

Momma took Declan's place next to me. I leaned my head on her shoulder. Even as an adult I still needed her, maybe now more than ever.

She patted my cheek. Her hand smelled like coconut oil.

"You're worried."

"Uh-huh."

"About what people will think or Declan?"

"All of the above."

"People are always going to talk, baby girl. And what comes out of their mouth says more about them than you."

"I'm not sure how comforting that is in light of the humiliation I've endured the last several months."

"But you have stood tall and true through it all. You walked the higher road. That speaks to your character."

"I'll admit, at times I've wanted revenge and vindication."

"The way you live your life is your vindication."

"People are going to think my marriage ended because of Declan."

"Then they don't know you well."

I lifted my head off her shoulder. "What if I don't know myself?"

Momma turned to me with narrowed eyes. "What do you mean, honey?"

"What if I'm making another mistake?"

"What was your first mistake?"

I tilted my head and widened my eyes. Wasn't that obvious? "Momma?"

Momma placed her hand on my abdomen. "This was not a mistake. Marrying Greyson wasn't a mistake. You made a choice, a good one as far as anyone could tell at the time. No one knows what the future holds." She looked at Declan and Daddy firing up the grill. "Could Declan break your heart? He could. Could your Daddy break mine? Yes. But then I would kill him." She laughed. "But honestly, he has broken my heart a time or two. I've broken his. That's life."

I raised my eyebrows, intrigued by this knowledge.

Momma smiled. "Your Daddy and I have been true to each other, but things get said and feelings get hurt. Doors have slammed and there have been nights we've gone to bed furious with one another. But the making up...now, that's worth the regret."

"You can stop there."

She laughed and leaned into me. "How do you think you got here?"

"Momma."

"After the little show you and Declan just put on, you don't need to pretend to be embarrassed."

I wasn't embarrassed, it's just I didn't look at my parents as sexual beings, and I didn't want to. "Thank you for interrupting us, by the way."

"That was your Daddy's idea."

Why didn't that surprise me? Momma and I leaned our heads together and watched the men.

"Just take it a day at a time, baby girl. You've been through a lot. And Declan's a good man, he'll wait."

"He seems a little impatient."

"Men get that way when they know exactly what they want, but it's okay to make them wait. It's good for them."

"I think he feels like he's been waiting for twelve years."

"That may be, but he made choices too."

Yes, he did.

∾

Social media was causing all sorts of trouble, and not only for me. Halle's mystery herbs were revealed, and it wasn't herbs at all, it was a shiny man by the name of Dr. Winters. I was beginning to question how smart he really was and if I wanted to put my baby's and my life in his hands.

How dumb do you have to be to date sisters, and identical twin sisters at that? I get that Heather moved on, but come on, you don't ask out the sister.

I had both sisters calling and texting me, each one upset.

It all started when several pictures from some comic book convention in Charleston posted photos of the event and Halle got tagged in some of them by her well-meaning friends from that world. She just happened to bring Dr. Dreamy with her. And well, Heather has a keen eye for these things and it came up in her Facebook feed, and the rest was history.

I decided this called for pedicures. My feet needed some TLC anyway. I was still trying to get all the dirt out from under my toenails. It was a good thing Declan's kisses made up for it.

Declan was wining and dining clients on Wednesday night so I decided to invite each sister out for a girl's night— they just didn't know they were both invited. It wasn't the first time I had been their referee and mediator, but this was the first time it was over a man. Heather was upset because Halle broke the no dating the same man rule that they had written in stone. Literally, it was. It was more like cement, but if you ever went to their parents' house and looked closely at the right corner of their patio you would see their pledge written with a popsicle stick right after the porch had been laid. Their parents were furious when they discovered it. You do crazy things when you're fourteen. Halle was upset because Heather was already dating Dr. Martin and obviously not interested in Dr. Winters. And she really, really liked Dr. Winters, from the way she gushed about him over the phone.

I had them meet me in Charleston since I was putting in some overtime getting first quarter numbers and reports finalized. First quarter had been good. I was analyzing costs and profit margins to make sure it stayed that way. And I wanted to make sure I had a handle on everything before I took time off when the baby came. I couldn't wait to get this little guy in my arms. It felt weird to ache for something you'd never experienced, but that's how I felt about my son.

I purposely arrived at the nail spa first so I could make sure they stayed when they both showed up separately. My plan was to send the first one in and tell them I had a call from Declan I had to take and would meet them in there. It could happen. He had already texted to say he missed me. I was missing his company too.

We hadn't seen a lot of each other the last few days. We were both busy with work. And last night I went to a breast-feeding class. I wasn't sure how to feel after it. It made it sound a lot more complicated than I thought it would be. I thought it was just going to be natural and the baby would take right to it, but so many seasoned moms and dads were in my class telling horror stories of cracked and bleeding nipples, clogged ducts, and fussy babies. And can I say how lonely it made me feel? Almost everyone brought a partner.

We all had to get up and introduce ourselves and give a little info about ourselves. So many of the women all mentioned how long they had been married and their partners were there smiling at them. I was tempted to get up and say, 'Hi, I'm Melanie, my husband left me, I live at home with my parents, I'm dating my boyfriend from high school, and I work for my daddy. You can find me crying in the corner wondering what I'm doing with my life.' Instead I went with, "Hi, I'm Melanie. I'm the CFO for a midsized commercial construction company and this is my first baby." It was all true, but I did wonder what I was doing with my life. And what would become of Declan and me.

I did love being with him, but I was in such a precarious time in my life. Declan didn't seem to mind, if anything he seemed excited about it. But how was he going to feel once the baby came and my chest was leaking breast milk all over the place, and I hadn't showered in three days because I was exhausted from staying up all night with a baby? I supposed I should ask him. So I did by text. I knew he probably had his phone off since he was with customers, but I had to get that out there.

Heather was first to arrive. Dr. Martin, or I guess I should say Sean, dropped her off. I pretended not to notice their long kiss goodbye, but it was hard since he drove a convertible and the top was down. He had taken her sailing. I hoped that meant she was in a good mood.

She was looking tan and windswept; the look worked well for her and she was all smiles. I needed to keep her that way. I knew she was going to be unhappy once she figured out Halle was invited too.

"You look fantastic." I hugged her.

She sighed. "I think I'm in love."

"Really? It's only been a few weeks."

"Fine, how about enraptured?"

"Whatever it is, it looks good on you."

"I know."

I rolled my eyes at her while pretending I was receiving a call. "Do you want to meet me inside? I need to take this call."

"Is it Declan?"

I grinned.

She laughed and walked in.

Phew. Halle was pulling into the parking lot. I met her at her car. She too looked happier than ever. She was sporting new purple-tipped hair. I loved her daring nature, at least when it came to her hair.

"I love the new do."

"Noah said it gives me a Cleopatra look."

I tossed my head from side to side. "I can see it."

"I think I'm going to get my toenails to match."

"I love it."

She placed her hand on my abdomen—she was one of the few people allowed to—as we headed in. "How are you feeling?"

"A little tired, but good."

We walked in and at first the sisters didn't notice each other. Heather was looking over the nail polish selection and Halle was still focused on me. It wasn't until Heather chose a color and turned around that the raven-haired beauties locked eyes. Each of their happy attitudes dissolved in seconds. I swore the temperature dropped, that's how cold the looks between the normally best of friend sisters were.

I took Halle's arm to make sure she didn't leave. She was a flight risk. I knew Heather would stay out of pure defiance.

The sisters hit me with their looks of displeasure.

I wasn't flinching. "I love you both and you love each other and we are going to have fun because pretty soon I'm going to smell like spit up, have breast milk squirting out of me uncontrollably, and maybe cracked and bleeding nipples. I'm not going to have time for pedicures."

They both laughed at me, but still wouldn't acknowledge each other.

"Was that a PSA for unintended pregnancies? Because if it wasn't it should be." Heather evilly grinned.

Halle scowled at her sister. "Her pregnancy wasn't unintended."

"I never said it was." Heather had her own nasty look for her sister. "It's a joke, but I forgot you don't know how to take one."

This sounded like a conversation they would have had back in middle school. "Ladies, remember we're here to have fun."

"Fine." Heather turned and stomped off to one of the empty pedicure chairs.

Halle and I picked out our nail polish color in silence before joining her. I ended up between them.

I wiggled my toes in the jetted bath for my feet and enjoyed the leg and foot massage given by the nail tech. Both of my friends seemed determined not to talk and I'm sure they were annoyed with me for tricking them, but their behavior was ridiculous and it was going to stop.

"Remember when I called you both after Greyson left me?"

That got their attention. They each set their phones down and looked my way.

"You both dropped what you were doing and drove straight through the night to be with me. The next day you stayed snuggled up on the couch with me between my morning sickness episodes. And you both made me smile despite the fact my world was falling apart. Those two women wouldn't let a man come between them." I directed my attention toward Heather. "Especially for a man that one of you doesn't care for."

Heather tried not to smile, but her defenses were weakening. She leaned over so she could see her sister. "Fine. I know. I guess I was irked because when I did go out with Noah, he was always asking about you."

Halle did her best to be gracious about that piece of news, but I could see in her eyes how pleased she was. "I really like him."

"He chews loudly." Heather grinned at her sister. That was her way of saying she was sorry.

"His mouth is usually otherwise engaged when we're together." Touché. I was proud of Halle. Even Heather looked impressed by her boldness. So much so we all started laughing.

"And you're a brat for tricking us." Heather smirked at me.

"You know you love me."

"By all the Facebook posts it looks like someone else does too," Heather replied.

That was still to be seen.

Chapter Fourteen

❦

I DROVE HOME WITH HAPPY, CLEAN FEET THAT LOOKED fabulous with pretty pink toenails. Halle and Heather made up and drove home together. I never heard back from Declan. I hope that meant his meeting was going well. Or maybe he was running scared from the earlier text. I mean, how many men really wanted to date a lactating zombie?

That's why I was surprised to see his truck in the drive when I arrived home. I pulled up behind him. He was out of his truck as soon as he saw me.

He opened my car door and helped me out. A smile danced in his eyes.

"What are you doing here?" I gazed up into his handsome face. I loved the five o'clock shadow he had going on.

He leaned in and brushed my lips. "I thought it would be better to respond to your message in person."

"I'm surprised you aren't running away."

He pushed me against the car and leaned in, careful of the precious cargo I carried. He trailed kisses up and down my neck. "If you're trying to get rid of me, it's not working," he breathed against my neck.

His touch had me tingling from head to toe. "I just want you to know what you're signing up for."

"Mel, I'm in this for the long haul. I'll make sure I always have extra t-shirts on hand for any breastmilk leaks. Besides, you look hot in my shirts, so I'm rooting for those."

I laughed into his chest.

He rubbed my back. "And if you ever need a nap, I'm your man. I'm up for baby duty anytime, day or night."

I looked up and peered into his sincere eyes. "Are you really sure?"

"Trust me."

"I want to."

"We'll keep working on it. But for now," he pulled my hand, "the cove and water are calling."

"The water is still cool at night this time of year."

"Believe me, you'll be plenty warm." His words alone sent a surge of heat through my body.

He didn't lie. I found myself wrapped up in him under a blanket of water. With each kiss, I found myself falling deeper and deeper for him. I ran my fingers through his thick, wet hair. He looked perfect under the glow of the moonlight. I loved the feel of his hand silkily falling down my arm leaving trails of raised skin as he went.

"I wish I would have never left you," he whispered.

"I wish you would have trusted me."

He leaned his forehead against mine. "Me too."

"Why didn't you believe me?"

He skimmed my lips. He tasted like saltwater and honey. "It never dawned on me you would say no. In my eighteen-year-old mind it didn't make sense. The only logical explanation was that there was someone else."

"And how was that logical? We were inseparable."

"I was eighteen."

"For a long time, I dreamed you would come for me."

He pulled me closer against his taut chest. "I thought about it all the time, but by the time I was smart enough, I figured it was too late. I heard you were serious with someone at Clemson."

I rested my head on his shoulder and let the waves lull us. "There's no looking back now."

"I want you to be able to trust me, Mel. I'm not that boy."

"You promised to be patient."

"Like I said, I'm not going anywhere."

He went on to prove that. But life meant to test us, as well.

❧

He started off with stopping by for a quick minute at work. Spring was a busy time of year for him and me. It was construction season. Daddy was gone more and more on site. He had taken me with him a few times, but he was more paranoid than me about my pregnancy, so he felt more comfortable with me in the office. And I didn't complain. I preferred the beautiful, clean, and climate controlled environment of our office over the trailers that didn't have adequate air conditioning this time of year. The days were getting warmer and more humid.

And I loved that Declan could pop in from time to time.

Today he came bearing a box and a smile.

I looked up from my laptop. "What's this? My birthday isn't until next week."

He carried over the box and set it on my desk. "Speaking of which, I do have some ideas, but do you have anything in mind?"

I loved that he asked. "Something low-key with just the two of us sounds perfect."

"I like the way you think."

I stood up to peek in the box. I laughed as I peered in. "Let me guess, you talked to your sister."

He looked so proud of himself. "Yes, ma'am." He started pulling out the items one by one. "She said these nursing pads are the best and prevent leaks, but I'm still holding out for you wearing my shirts. Here's some cream, she said it prevents cracking. She likes this pump and said it was a lifesaver. I didn't even know you could pump." He set it aside before pulling out a couple of books and handing them to me. "She said these were the best purchases of her life, that she learned more from them than she ever learned in any class."

I didn't even look them over. I set them down and met him on the other side of my desk. I grabbed his shirt and pulled him to me.

His grin said he was hoping that would happen.

"I think I may be falling in love with you, Declan Shaw." That just came falling out of my mouth, but it was true.

He brushed his hand through my hair. "I never stopped loving you." He pressed his lips against mine.

I pulled away from him. "Do you really love me?"

He nodded, but it was his eyes that shouted yes.

A single tear ran down my cheek.

He kissed my forehead. "I wish I could stay, but I have to get to an appointment. What time is your class over tonight?"

I sighed. I was debating on whether to go or not. They kind of depressed me. "I think nine."

He cocked his head. "What's wrong?"

"Nothing."

"That's not true."

"It's just that going to these classes is a glaring reminder that I'm a single parent."

"You're not single." He pulled me to him. "And all you have to do is say the word and I'll go with you. I'll even be there in the delivery room with you if you want me to."

I bit my lip. I had thought about asking but…"What if we break up? And you realize the kind of things that go on in a delivery room, right? It goes way beyond leaked breastmilk."

"First of all, we aren't breaking up." He rested his hand on my abdomen. "And I want to experience this with you. I want to be the one holding your hand. I want to be there when this little man takes his first breath."

I rested my hand on his cheek. "I'm going to make you late if you keep talking like that."

He groaned. "Don't tempt me. Text me the address where the class is held and I'll meet you there."

I nodded, too choked up to speak.

He bent down and kissed my belly. "Be good for your mom, try to stay out of her ribs, and lay off the heartburn."

I laughed and ran my fingers through his hair.

He stood up and kissed me hard once. "I'll see you later."

He didn't know how much I looked forward to it.

But I wasn't sure how much he was looking forward to the delivery room scene after the first birthing class and the videos they showed of real deliveries. While I was in awe with the power and wonderment of the female body, he whispered in my ear, "It reminds me of the movie *Alien.*"

He was all in, though, when it came time to learn massage techniques to help me through contractions. And when one of the husbands in the class raised his hand and asked the instructor, "I read that making out and caressing your wife during labor can help. Is that true?"

His wife's eyes about bulged out and she smacked him.

The instructor, to my surprise, validated the husband. "There have been studies that show that intense kissing can help stimulate and even help labor progress."

The men in the class all erupted in a collective grin, even the one I brought.

"I think we should test this theory out." Declan kissed the side of my head.

I didn't know if that was going to happen, but having him by my side at class that night meant the world to me. Knowing that I had someone to count on that was only there for me was a life changing moment. I knew my friends would have been there, but now that Halle and my doctor were dating, that was a no go, and Heather and my doctor in the same room was probably not a good call at this time.

I knew Declan would be drama free.

But little did I know the drama life had in store for us.

Chapter Fifteen

THIRTY. I WAS THIRTY. I COULD REMEMBER WHEN I thought thirty was ancient. It made me reflect on where I was versus where I thought I would be. Life really hadn't turned out the way I planned, but I had hit some of my goals. I was making the salary I figured I would be at this age, thank you Daddy. I was having my first baby, though I had wanted one with one on the way at this age. I had owned a home, but obviously not anymore. I still needed to work on that, but between Declan and work I had let that fall to the wayside. Besides, I was interested in seeing where Declan would buy.

I thought he had decided on building, but a few days ago he asked me if it was a wise financial decision to borrow money against your 401k for a down payment. It could be if it was a solid investment, but it was always risky because the housing market fluctuated so much. I was surprised he asked, because he had made it sound like between his first quarter bonus and savings he would have over ten percent to put down on the house he was looking at. When I pressed for more details, his response was he was looking at all his options.

Being thirty coincided with being just over thirty weeks pregnant. The baby and I were on track. I was still deciding on names. Nothing spoke to me. The baby had his own language. He was most active in the middle of the day and evening. I think he was going to be a soccer player because he had some powerful kicks. He seemed to like Declan, too. Every time Declan talked to him or felt him, this little guy moved. Or maybe it was his mother's increased heart rate.

Declan had a way with getting my blood pumping. Like when I came home on my birthday thinking I was getting ready for Declan to pick me up for dinner, and instead I found him in the backyard near the pool. He and Momma were putting the finishing touches on dinner for two. Momma scurried away as soon as I arrived. She wore a pleased looked as she kissed my cheek and wished me a good night and happy birthday. Momma, Daddy, and I had had lunch together earlier to celebrate.

Did I mention Declan was in swimming trunks? My blood was definitely pumping. His tan skin glistened in the evening sun. He took my hand and led me to the set table. "I hope you don't mind an evening at home?"

"Not at all." I took in every one of his muscles.

He smiled at my apparent admiration for him. "You'll be changing after dinner. I prefer your white suit, by the way." He pulled out my chair for me and kissed my neck. "Happy birthday."

"Thank you. This looks incredible." I looked over the pasta salad and skewers of grilled steak and vegetables. Not to mention my favorite, strawberry cheesecake.

"As do you." He kissed my neck again for good measure.

"Thanks for lying. I noticed some swelling in my ankles today."

He sat down across from me. "You are gorgeous, swollen ankles and all."

"You still have time to run."

"Not a chance." He held up his flute of sparkling cider. "To many more birthdays together."

He made sure everything was perfect for the night, right down to the lit floating candles in the pool at dusk.

"It's settled." He led me into the pool while his eyes roved over my very pregnant body. "I'm getting a place with a pool."

I smiled and shook my head at him. "How you find me attractive right now, I have no idea."

He pulled me to him in the water. "You've never been sexier."

"Are you kidding me? You knew me when I didn't have an ounce of fat on my body."

He ran his hand down the length of my body. "Melanie Dixon, I love every curve on you. Even pregnant you have a better body than most."

I ran my hand up his defined chest. "I think I'm going to keep you around."

He groaned before his lips landed on mine and stayed that way for a good pleasurable hour. It was the best birthday ever, until…

Abruptly Declan's lips glided off mine and his body tensed. A cold stare replaced his passionate gaze.

"What's wrong?"

He flicked his head and I turned around in his arms. Shock didn't even begin to cover how I felt. I hadn't even heard the patio door open above the noise of the pool's waterfall we were near, much less heard anyone walk out. "Greyson," I gasped.

Declan's arms tightened around me.

Daddy stood next to Greyson looking like he might take

a swing at my ex-husband. "Baby girl, I'm sorry to interrupt you. He insisted on seeing you." Daddy wouldn't even say his name.

Greyson stood proud, wearing a business casual look. His dark tousled hair blew in the sea air. He acted like he was doing his best to look as unaffected as possible by the scene in front of him. But I noticed the fire in his eyes directed at Declan.

"What are you doing here?" I stammered.

"It's important I speak to you."

"We don't have anything to say to each other."

"We have some unfinished business."

I couldn't think of anything. "Then your lawyer should contact mine."

"This is of a personal nature."

"Divorcing me felt pretty personal, so again, contact my lawyer." I felt Declan steadying me.

In the low light, I could see Greyson's brow furrow like it always did when he was frustrated. "Please, it's important." It's the closest to begging he had ever been.

I turned and met Declan's rage filled eyes, which softened for me.

"You don't have to talk to him."

"I know." But I was going to hear what he had to say out of sheer curiosity.

Declan and I swam to the edge of the pool. Declan got out first before helping me out and handing me a towel. I wrapped up in the warm cotton. It felt good against my skin. Declan took my hand and we walked together toward Greyson and his formidable presence.

Daddy's eyes were filled with concern. "Are you okay, darlin'?"

"I'm fine. Why don't you go in the house?" I was afraid his blood pressure was going to boil over.

"Are you sure?"

I nodded.

Daddy left, but not before giving Declan the 'you better handle this' signal. Declan looked up for the challenge.

With Daddy gone, Greyson kept his focus on Declan, in particular Declan's tattoo. "I'd like to speak to Melanie alone."

"That's not going to happen." Declan wrapped his arm around me.

I took comfort in his touch.

"I don't know who you are, but—"

"I'll tell you who I am—" Unadulterated hate was coming off my normally sweet and mild mannered Declan.

"Let's stop this right now," I intervened. I looked into Declan's simmering eyes. "Give me a few minutes." I knew that wasn't going to go over well, and I saw the hurt in his eyes. "Please, trust me." I kissed his lips once.

Declan let out a tense breath. "Always."

I gave him a small smile. "I won't be long."

Declan kissed my head before giving Greyson a scathing look. "Tread carefully," he warned.

I watched him walk away, wishing he didn't have to but knowing it was for the best. I knew Greyson well enough to know he wasn't going anywhere until he had his say.

Greyson's gray eyes fixed on my baby bump. I wasn't really showing the last time we saw each other and this was the first time since he left me that he had really looked at me.

"How are you feeling?"

"Do you really care?"

"I do."

His answer caught me off guard. "You can have a seat." I pointed to one of the cushioned patio chairs.

We both took a seat next to each other.

"Why are you here? I don't think it's to wish me a happy birthday."

"It is your birthday. I forgot."

"It wouldn't be the first time."

His jaw tightened. "I suppose I could have been a better husband."

"You suppose?"

"What do you want me to say? I screwed up? You deserved better?"

"I did deserve better."

"You seemed to have moved on quickly."

"That's none of your business and frankly insulting coming from someone who cheated on me."

He ran his hands through his hair and leaned forward. "Melanie, I didn't come here to argue with you. Despite what you may believe, I am sorry."

I scoffed.

He looked up and met my eyes. "I don't expect you to believe me."

I didn't. "So you came to apologize?"

"I came to talk to you. Some things have happened that you need to be aware of."

I narrowed my eyes at him. I was more than confused. "Our lives have been severed. Forever. You made sure of that."

His eyes landed on my baby. "You're carrying my son."

"No." I felt panicked. "You signed away your rights."

"I did, but my mother didn't."

"She did when she believed your lies."

He stood up and paced in front of me. Agitation marked

his every step. "I'm under investigation and I've been asked to hand in my resignation."

This was almost more stunning than him showing up here. "What did you do?"

His anger-filled eyes bore into me. "It wasn't me."

My gaze back said to enlighten me.

"Anya..."

My skin crawled hearing her name. I remembered her slinking herself over Greyson at our divorce hearing.

"She was stealing money from the bank and our relationship came to light."

"Maybe you shouldn't have brought her to court with you." I smirked with satisfaction.

He looked out into the distance. "It wasn't the best idea."

"What does any of this have to do with me?"

"Don't be surprised if you get a call from the state regulators and the board of directors."

"I hope you don't expect me to tell them what a stand-up guy you are."

"I don't expect anything from you. I'm just letting you know so you aren't surprised."

"How courteous of you."

He threw himself back in the chair next to me. "I know you hate me, but you know I would never jeopardize my job or the bank."

"Believe me, I know how much you loved both. Are we done here?"

He rubbed his hand across his face and blew out a deep breath. "You got to be too much."

I whipped my head toward him. "What does that mean?"

"You knew who I was when you married me. I never promised you a white-picket-fence marriage."

"And I never asked for one. But you did promise me your fidelity."

He turned away from me. "I came home to you every night."

"And that made it okay?"

"No. But you wanted more of me than I could give."

"So it's my fault?"

His silence filled the air.

"Did you ever love me?"

He slowly turned his head my direction. The patio lights reflected in his eyes. He swallowed. "I still love you."

My eyes widened in disbelief.

"I know that doesn't matter now. I didn't come here for me. My mother wants to know her grandchild."

I felt ill inside. "If you even think about taking me to court…"

"I wouldn't do that to you."

The knot loosened in my chest.

"I'm asking you to talk to her. She's here. We're staying at the beachside cottages."

"You both have a lot of nerve coming here after everything you put me through."

"I realize that and so does she. My mistakes snowballed and now I'm paying the price. Please don't punish her…she's not in good health."

"What's wrong?"

"Her cancer has returned and she's refusing treatment."

I knew she'd had colon cancer several years ago before I ever entered the picture.

"The treatment for her is worse than the cure, but she wants to get to know her grandson before she dies." Emotion crept into his voice.

Nothing like a little guilt. "I'll think about it."

"Thank you." He stood up to leave.

I knew this was the last chance to ask him the lingering question in my mind. "What do I tell my son about you?"

His gray eyes hit me with such force. It wasn't the first time I had felt their effect. "Tell him I will always regret never getting to know him."

Chapter Sixteen

≈≈≈

HAPPY BIRTHDAY TO ME. I TOOK REFUGE IN DECLAN'S ARMS the remainder of the night on the sunroom couch. I lay with my head in his lap, him stroking my hair. My parents had gone to bed upset, especially Momma. She didn't want Tamara anywhere near me or my baby. Part of me felt that way too, but I used to have great love and admiration for my ex-mother-in-law. And now to hear she was dying caused a dizzying set of emotions to whirl inside of me.

"Do you ever think I'm too much?"

He stopped stroking my hair. "No. I can't get enough of you."

I drew closer to him.

"I love you, Mel." He began stroking my hair again.

"I know."

"I'm sorry if I acted like I was going to pee on you to mark my territory."

That got me to laugh. "Thank you for not going that route."

"I've never wanted to throw a punch more in my life."

"I could tell."

"What are you going to do?"

"That's a good question. Tamara has invited me to their cottage tomorrow night for dinner."

I felt Declan tense.

"If I go, would you come with me?"

He immediately relaxed.

I turned over so I could look up into his face. It wasn't as easy as it used to be. "You know I'm not in love with Greyson anymore, right?"

He ran his finger down my cheek. "I could see in his eyes he's still in love with you, and even though he's terminated his legal rights to your baby, the fact remains, you will always be connected to him through your son."

"And this bothers you."

"Not for the reasons you think."

"Then tell me."

"Mel, you don't know how much I wish you were carrying our child. How much I regret our years apart. I'll love your son like my own; I just hope he'll feel the same way."

I reached up and rested my hand on his cheek. "Declan Shaw, this baby is going to think the world of you, just like his mother."

He took my hand and kissed the inside of it. "If you want to meet them for dinner, I'll go with you."

"No peeing on me, okay?"

He wrapped me up in his arms, laughing. "I make no promises."

I lay in bed that night thinking about what I should do. My conscience was being a nuisance. It kept reminding me of all the shopping and lunch dates I'd had with Tamara. How she nursed me back to health on occasion when I was sick. And how she treated me like the daughter she never had. But it was hard to forget her turning her back on me.

Then I thought about what kind of person I really was, and what I wanted to teach my son. Did I want to be vindictive or forgiving? I couldn't be both.

In the end that made my decision for me. I wanted my son to be kind and forgiving and that started with me. It didn't mean that I had to agree with what she had done, but for my own sake I needed to forgive her. And she was dying. That hit me harder than I thought it would under the circumstances.

I thought about Greyson too. I wanted to take more pleasure in the fact that he was getting his just desserts. Don't get me wrong, there was a part of me that felt like he deserved it and maybe I was a tad happy in that evil sort of way, but I knew how much he loved his mother and I felt sorry for him.

But most of all I thought of Declan and how much I loved him. How I think I never stopped loving him. We just hit the pause button for an extended period of time. No one had ever made me feel so loved or wanted.

And did I ever need him as we drove down Seaside Boulevard to the cottages Dallas Harper owned. Declan rubbed his thumb across my hand while he drove. "What are you thinking?"

"That I'm crazy for doing this."

"I'm going to agree with you."

"Thanks." I smiled over at him. "And I'm kind of bummed."

"What about?"

"The red bungalow is under contract."

"I told you to go look at it."

"It was so expensive."

"You're telling me."

I narrowed my eyes at him. "How do you know?"

He cleared his throat. "I looked it up after you talked about it so much."

"Oh. It's nice, isn't it?"

"Very nice."

I sighed.

He squeezed my hand. "I'm sorry you're bummed, but I have a feeling we'll both end up in the right place."

"I can't think about it until after the baby comes and I get through this dinner. Thank you for coming with me."

"I wouldn't be anywhere else."

"Please make sure to check the testosterone at the door."

"Now, baby, what fun would that be?"

"I think fun is the last thing that will be happening tonight."

"Says you. We're going to pick up where we left off last night in the pool."

"That was fun. And my parents go to bed early." I sounded like I was in high school again.

He wagged his eyebrows. "Even better."

The playful talk helped calm my nerves, but they crept back up when we arrived at the resort.

Declan held me close as we headed toward the yellow cottage. The resort had several cottages, all in bright colors. Of course, Greyson rented one of the larger ones. I had to hand it to Dallas, he had done a nice job with the resort. It looked like the place was booked, which was saying something considering tourist season wasn't in full swing yet.

The smell of barbecue wafted on the breeze while the sound of couples playing at the beach filled in for background noise. Though it couldn't mask the pounding of my heart. I thought I was done with this part of my life. I was moving on. I had found love again.

We arrived sooner than I was ready, but I was never going to be ready. I took a steadying breath before we walked up the wooden steps to the small porch of the yellow-shingled cottage. Declan knocked for us. It was a good thing as I was having thoughts of leaving. He kissed my head for reassurance.

Greyson answered the door within seconds. He was on the phone. Shocker. He waved us in, scowling at Declan. He walked into the kitchen jabbering away about business as per his usual.

I locked eyes with Tamara and took in the aroma of her prized chicken piccata. She knew how much I loved that dish and how I could never quite master her recipe. Her azure eyes looked as worried as I felt. I could tell she had lost some weight. Her wrinkled skin was sagging more than the last time I had seen her, but her gray hair and makeup were flawless as usual.

We both seemed at a loss for words. I was grateful for Declan stepping in. "I'm Declan, ma'am." He held his hand out to her. I knew how difficult that must have been for him, but it made me love him all the more.

Her aged, manicured hand took his. She was the picture of elegance and grace. I had always admired that about her. "It's a pleasure to meet you." She didn't sound so sure. She dropped his hand quickly and focused back on me and the ever-growing belly under my black blouse.

"Tamara." I found the courage to speak.

Hurt filled her eyes. I used to call her mom. She stepped closer. "Melanie, you look radiant."

"Thank you."

She looked like she wanted to embrace me, but held off. I appreciated that. "Dinner is ready to be served."

Normally that was good news, but nerves had me feeling a little queasy. I smiled anyway.

"Do you mind eating out on the patio?" Tamara asked. "I love the view."

"Not at all," I answered for us.

We followed her back through the furnished cottage, styled in an aquatic theme. We had to pass through the kitchen where Greyson was still engaged in conversation to get to the patio door.

"Greyson." Tamara meant business. "Please get off the phone. I would like your help serving."

I could never have gotten away with that, at least not without receiving a cold stare, but for his mother he easily complied.

Declan and I slipped out. Normally, I would have offered to help, but this felt surreal to me and they weren't my favorite people anymore.

Declan helped me into the wrought iron chair and took the one next to me around the round umbrellaed table. The breeze was picking up and the salt in the air lingered.

"You okay?" Declan checked in with me.

"I'm ready for this to be over."

"Me too. I'm not exactly feeling loved here."

I leaned in and kissed his cheek. "I'll make it up to you."

"I can't wait."

Our brief moment alone ended when Greyson and Tamara walked out with the food. Uncomfortable silence hung in the air.

I took Declan's hand under the table.

Greyson looked as unhappy as I'd ever seen him.

Tamara was pensive. "I hope you still love chicken piccata?" She set a salad bowl on the table.

I nodded that I did.

She let out a breath and took a seat next to Declan, leaving Greyson to sit by me. So awkward, but I had a feeling Tamara did it on purpose. She was barking up a tree that had been chopped down and run through a wood chipper.

"Please help yourself." Tamara waved at the spread.

No one moved for what seemed like an eternity, but it couldn't have been more than thirty seconds.

"I know this is under less than ideal circumstances, but please." Tamara pleaded with me.

I reached for a roll. "Thank you for dinner. It looks wonderful."

That seemed to give everyone else permission to fill up their plates.

"So Declan," Greyson said his name with such vitriol, "what do you do for a living?"

Declan set his glass of water down. "I'm the district manager for a large heavy equipment vendor."

"How many people do you oversee?"

"Everyone in the Charleston and nearby areas." Declan was getting annoyed.

"Where did you go to school?" Here we go. Greyson had to make sure Declan knew he was a Harvard graduate.

"Undergrad at Virginia Tech. MBA from Columbia."

"Not as good as Harvard's, but passable."

I placed my hand on Declan's leg hoping he wouldn't play Greyson's game. "And I went to Clemson and I'm a CFO. Will you please pass the salad dressing?" I asked Tamara.

She grinned as she handed it to me, I'm sure in response to my previous statement. "Where are you working now?"

"I'm working for my dad."

"Construction company, right?" Tamara seemed pleased she remembered.

"Yes."

"I suppose that means you two see each other often?" Greyson grimaced.

"As often as we can." Declan smirked at Greyson.

"And how did you two meet?" Greyson wasn't letting it drop.

"Please, can we stop this? Greyson, Declan and I are none of your business."

"There's more than you to consider." Greyson stared at midsection.

"You walked away." My blood was boiling. "And Declan has been more of a father to my baby than you ever would have been."

Declan held my hand like a vice.

Greyson pushed away from the table. "We'll never know now, will we?" He stalked off into the cottage.

Tamara's eyes welled up with tears. "He's having a harder time letting go than he thought he would."

That brought me no comfort whatsoever. "I think we should go."

"Melanie, please give me a few more moments of your time."

I met her tear-filled eyes. "Tamara, I don't know what you want from me. You pushed me and my son out of your life, not to mention how you humiliated me and left me alone when I needed you more than ever."

Her shoulders began to shake. "You don't know how sorry I am for that," she cried.

Her tears and frail exterior made me feel awful.

Declan wisely stood. "I'm going to give you two a moment alone. If you need me, Mel, I'll be right past the dunes." He kissed my head.

I took his vacated seat so I could be closer to Tamara.

Tamara watched him walk away. "Do you love him?"

"Very much."

Her face fell in disappointment. "We've missed you."

"I find that hard to believe."

She reached out her hand and rested it on my arm. "If I could undo the past several months, I would."

I used to think that way too, but I was happier with Declan than I had ever been with Greyson. "I'm happy."

"I see that in your eyes."

I nodded awkwardly. "I'm sorry to hear about your illness."

"We all have to go sometime." She rubbed my arm. "But I can't go until we make amends."

"That's going to take some time."

"That's why I'm staying here."

Wow. That was quite the twist in the plot. I hope that didn't mean that her son was staying.

"I haven't told Greyson yet, but I could do with some sea air and a change of scenery. And," she looked longingly at my baby, who was kicking me in the ribs. "I want to meet that grandson of mine." Tears rolled down her cheek. "And I miss my daughter."

What did I say to that?

Chapter Seventeen

TAMARA'S PRESENCE ADDED A WHOLE NEW DYNAMIC AND A new round of gossip in the Indigo Bay world. Now Miss Lucille had me in a bitter custody battle with my ex-husband, and Declan was a charlatan for trying to tear us apart.

I promised Greyson I would watch out for Tamara. It wasn't my first choice, but what could I do? She was staying and her doctor was giving her a year to live. I wasn't heartless.

It caused some tension though. Momma wasn't happy. Daddy was livid. Declan worried that this was Greyson's way of interfering with our relationship and trying to work his way back into my life. I wasn't too worried about that. I knew I wasn't Greyson's true or even first love. And he was fighting for his position at the bank tooth and nail from what Tamara said. Work was his mistress long before Anya came into the picture. She was probably regretting that now. Greyson was making sure she was prosecuted to the full letter of the law.

And real life seemed to kick in, making the days and weeks a blur of meetings, proposals, doctor's appointments, and birthing classes. I actually enjoyed those because it meant I got to see Declan. He was doing a lot of traveling around the state during the week doing trainings, but he always made sure he was in town Wednesday night for my class.

"You're going to be here for the birth, right?" I got that out in between practicing my breathing techniques.

"I made sure next week is the last week of trainings. I wouldn't miss it for the world. Just don't go into labor early." He grinned.

I looked down at my thirty-six-week belly. "He's going to have to vacate soon. I'm huge."

Declan, who I was leaning against, reached around and ran his hands over my abdomen. "You're beautiful. And he needs to cook a little longer."

"I've missed you. You've been a little distant the last few weeks."

He paused, making my heart hiccup.

"Are you rethinking us?"

"Never. I just wanted to give you some space with Tamara in town. And I've been working on some stuff."

I turned my head. "What stuff?"

He kissed my lips. "Important stuff."

"Are you going to tell me?"

"Uh-huh." He nodded. "But not tonight." His crooked smile made an appearance.

I turned back around and focused back on my breathing. "I didn't want to know anyway."

He laughed in my ear. "Sure you do. And when I'm done, you'll be the first person to know." He kissed my cheek. "I love you."

"I suppose I love you too."

"I love it when you say that, but I need a little more enthusiasm to go with it."

"I'm as big as a house in the middle of the summer. This is about as enthusiastic as I get."

He wrapped his arms around me. "I don't have to leave until tomorrow morning, so what do you say to the pool and a massage?"

"I think I can muster up some enthusiasm to thank you."

He groaned against my ear. "Do you want to leave now?"

I leaned my head against him. "Thank you for being so good to me. What can I do for you?"

"You're doing it already. Just keep taking care of yourself and this baby. I hate being away from you right now."

"I can do that."

Our time apart was giving me the opportunity to spend more time with my family and friends, Tamara included. Though that was difficult because Momma was not in a very forgiving mood when it came to Greyson's mom. I had to beg her to invite Tamara to the baby shower next weekend. It's not like Tamara and I were the best of friends again, but she was trying her best to make amends and she was running out of time.

Greyson had hired a private nurse to watch over her while she was here. Dallas offered long-term rentals at his resort so she was staying in the same yellow cottage. I spent some of my free evenings with her playing cards and taking walks on the beach if she felt up to it. It was tenuous and sometimes quiet, but it was getting less awkward. She liked to tell me stories about being a new mother. I did my best to ignore that her baby was my ex-husband. I even laughed when she recounted tales of Greyson being able to strip down to nothing in a second flat and run down the aisles of the grocery store. Or how she had to call the police because she thought he was missing, but he was quietly hiding under a decorative table covered by a tablecloth. She obviously enjoyed motherhood and missed the days of years gone by.

Momma and her best friend, Karen, were throwing the baby shower of the century on my behalf, and to my chagrin it was getting out of control. I had to put my foot down when Momma suggested live entertainment. I didn't need to be serenaded by the cute local pop band.

What I needed was to have this baby. My back was killing me and there were days when I couldn't wear shoes because of my swollen feet. And I was exhausted. This baby was sucking the life right out of me. Dr. Dreamy said I was anemic, so that explained it, but the iron supplements didn't seem to be helping. But more than anything, I just wanted to meet this little guy. Even if I didn't know what I should name him. Daddy was still angling for me to name him after him, and that was a possibility. I also liked the name Austin. Austin Dixon sounded nice, but what if I got married? It was probably too soon to think about that, and Declan hadn't mentioned the "M" word, even though he talked like we were a forever sort of thing. I mean, he was going to be in the delivery room with me. If that didn't say commitment I don't know what did.

I woke up the day of the baby shower, thirty-seven weeks along. I didn't feel all that good. I hadn't slept well. My back had ached so bad I soaked in the tub for an hour during the middle of the night. I needed Declan's magic hands. I hadn't seen him all week. He sent me a quick text to let me know he was home and safe late last night. I wasn't sure when I was going to see him. He said he was going to be busy this weekend working on "things." It had me feeling uneasy. Call it pregnancy hormones or insecurity, I kept wondering if maybe I was "too much," like Greyson accused me of being. Now Declan felt the same way, he just didn't want to say anything in my condition.

With my body and mind not in the best place, I had to face the baby shower.

Momma was going so overboard she bought me an outfit specifically for the occasion. It matched the decorations. How precious was this thing going to get? I was so tired of maternity clothes, I was planning on burning them when this was all said and done. But the mint summer dress was cute, even if I did feel like a whale in everything I wore.

I told Tamara I would pick her up and we would drive over to Karen's together. She lived down the road on the same stretch of coast as us. She and Momma could have been twins. They both had red hair and perky attitudes. At least Momma's was mostly perky. She wasn't thrilled that Tamara was coming. I begged her to be nice.

I felt so off that I didn't eat much at breakfast.

"You all right, baby girl?" Daddy cocked his head. Momma had already left for Karen's.

I rubbed my lower back. "Just tired. Do you think you could set the crib up in my room today?"

"Sure, darlin'. I'll ask Declan to help when he drops by later."

My head popped up. "Why is Declan coming over?" And why didn't he tell me?

"Said he had some business to discuss." Daddy grinned. "He wants us to use him exclusively."

"Oh."

"Baby girl, what's wrong?"

"Nothing." I choked back the tears.

Daddy set down his tablet. "Honey, something's off. What's going on?"

That opened up the flood gates. "I'm as big as a cow, everything is swollen, I'm tired, and I think Declan wants to break up with me."

Daddy had that deer in the headlights look that most men get when a woman gets emotional. He recovered though. He stood up and pulled me up and into a hug. He rubbed my back. "Darlin', you're talking nonsense."

"No, I'm not. Look at me. And Declan's been avoiding me."

"You're beautiful. And honey, it's the nature of his job, not you."

"That's what I thought about Greyson."

Daddy tensed. "He's no Greyson."

"How do we know? Maybe it's me."

He took my puffy face in his hands. "Melanie Jane Dixon, I don't want to hear you talk like that. Any man would be lucky to have you."

"You have to say that."

He kissed my forehead. "I've been chasing away boys and men from you for longer than I care to remember. No one has as good of a heart as you. And I've never met a smarter, more capable woman. And you're as pretty as a sunset."

"You're so biased." I clung to him.

"I know of what I speak. You're tired. You need to slow down."

"I need to get the second quarter reports done."

He laughed. "You need to put a smile on that face and show up at your momma's shower." Daddy knew who it was really for.

"I'll try."

He kissed my head once more. "And don't worry about Declan."

That was going to be easier said than done.

Chapter Eighteen

I DID MY BEST TO PUT ON A HAPPY FACE AMONG WHAT FELT like the whole town of Indigo Bay. But Declan lingered in my mind. Why did he have time to visit Daddy and not me? And what was he working on? Maybe it was another woman? Was I so naïve to fall for the whole "I'm busy with work" line again?

And don't even get me going on how over the top this shower was. Momma and Karen went with a *Jungle Book* theme. They had vines strung across Karen's great room and huge life-size stuffed animals. Where Momma thought I was going to put those I had no idea. The cake was as big as a wedding cake with an elephant on the top. Then there was the huge pile of gifts. It was embarrassing. Momma and Tamara were in some type of unspoken competition and I think their gifts made up half of the pile.

Halle and Heather smirked next to me and did their best not to laugh. They knew this was not my thing.

It only got better when Miss Lucille showed up in her Sunday finest wearing red beads and shoes, her white fluffy dog in a matching red collar. She sat like the Queen of Sheba next to Tamara, like a hawk diving in for the kill. I wanted to intervene but it was too late.

Tamara sat stoically in her designer clothes taking it all in. I felt bad for her and did try to talk to her, as well as have Halle and Heather throw her some attention. I knew she was in an uncomfortable situation, but I had to admire her tenacity.

Miss Lucille took her hand like she was some benevolent creature. "I must say that I'm surprised to see you here."

Tamara pulled her hand away. "Do I know you?"

Miss Lucille's face wore a smile worthy of any politician. "Where are my manners? I'm Lucille Sanderson. And I just have to say that I admire your selfless attitude in attending what I'm sure is a painful reminder for you of," she leaned in as if she was trying to be discreet, "Melanie's betrayal."

My raging hormones were about to be let loose, especially as everyone around us was now honed in on the conversation. But to my surprise, I didn't have to say a word.

Tamara sat up proud. "You seem to have left your manners at home. You would do well not to speak about things you have no idea of. And I would caution you to speak better of my daughter-in-law." Tamara met my eyes. They were looking a little blurry. She still thought of me as her family.

I gave her my best smile. I noticed even Momma give her a tender look.

Miss Lucille stood up with her pooch. "Well, I just remembered I have an appointment to get to."

Heather and Halle laughed as we watched her go. She had more swing in her hips than a playground. And thankfully everyone was so used to her that they went right back to eating and talking like it never happened.

I reached over and grabbed Tamara's hand. "Thank you."

She patted my hand. "It's I who should thank you, my dear."

Our relationship was nowhere near where it was. I wasn't sure it ever could be, but I was glad something remained between us.

Momma had me sit in the middle of all the ladies while I opened my gifts. I didn't like being the center of attention in my current condition. My back was killing me and I couldn't find a comfortable position. I also felt nauseated. Not to mention my mental state of mind. I had almost convinced myself Declan and I were over. Holding back my tears was becoming harder and harder. Yet there Momma stood with a camera, and after every gift I opened I had to smile for a picture. I was going to find a way to delete all those photos. When I said I felt as big as a cow, I meant it. No need for photographic evidence.

By the thirtieth gift, I'd had enough. I was more than grateful for everyone's generosity—this kid was going to have enough clothes and diapers to last us for eternity—but all I wanted was to sit in a bath or take a nap. Or maybe just talk to Declan. I needed to know one way or the other how he felt.

In a matter of seconds, my inner desire was answered. The doorbell rang and before I knew it, Declan had joined the party dressed up in slacks and my favorite blue button-up that brought out his eyes. In his hand, he held two small white bags.

My heart rushed and worried all at the same time.

Every woman's attention was directed toward him.

"Sorry to crash the party, ladies, but I wanted to give Mel my gifts for her and the baby."

Momma swooned with her hand across her heart along with all the other women around me, except for maybe Halle and Heather who were too wrapped up in their own relationships.

Declan, though, only had eyes for me. He approached and kneeled in front of me. He set the bags next to him. He took my hand in his. "Melanie Dixon, I just talked to your dad, and it sounds like I need to clear up your misconceptions about my feelings for you."

His smile and touch warmed me. The tears that had been threatening finally shed.

His hand came up and caressed my wet cheek. "From the first moment I laid eyes on you, I knew you were the girl for me. Our time apart only proved it to me. I love you. I've always loved you." He reached down and picked up one of the bags and handed it to me. "I hope this will cast out any doubts you may have."

With shaky hands, I took the bag and looked inside. A black velvet box rested on cellophane. The tears flowed more freely when I reached in and took out the small box.

Declan did the honors and opened it. There sat the most stunning rose gold diamond ring, at least I was pretty sure that's what I saw through my tears and a contraction. Yes, I said contraction. I did my best to hide it. I didn't want to ruin the moment.

Declan removed the beautiful ring from the box. He was trying to force it on my swollen finger. "Melanie Jane Dixon, will you marry me?"

Gasps and oohs and ahhs rang in the room.

I did my best to focus on an expectant Declan. My heart was saying yes, but all my body could do was think of the pain coursing through it. And then it happened. "Declan," I barely managed to get out. I forgot how to breath.

His anxious eyes locked with mine.

"My water broke." At least I hoped that's what it was. If not, I was going to really be embarrassed.

A flurry of activity broke out around me. Momma, Tamara, Halle, and Heather all rushed to my side knocking poor Declan out of the way. They were all touching me—like that was going to help—and making plans on what to do with me like I wasn't there.

I finally came to my senses enough to realize all that had happened in the moment. I took a deep cleansing breath. "Declan."

He parted the sea of women to get to me.

"Will you take me to the hospital? We need to stop by the house and grab my bag and we need to call the doctor." We had planned and practiced this.

Declan took charge and asked for some towels before helping me out to his truck.

All the women followed us out saying they would meet us at the hospital.

"Any contractions?" Declan asked, we had almost made it to his truck.

I nodded.

He helped me in and got me situated on the towels. I had never felt more uncomfortable in my life, but happiness filled me. I was finally going to meet my little man.

Declan brought an air of calm and comfort as we headed toward the hospital. Momma said she would grab my bag.

Declan reached over and took my hand. "Not to put any pressure on you, but you never answered my question."

I looked down at the mostly put on ring that my finger bore. It was beautiful, with eternity strands filled with diamonds and one large round-cut diamond in the middle. I couldn't have picked out a better ring myself. "Are you sure?"

He rubbed his thumb across my hand. "Mel, you're the only one for me."

I felt the truth of his words in my soul. "I would be honored to be your wife." Tears blurred my eyes.

Tears filled his eyes too. "Phew. I was worried there for a minute we were going to have a repeat of the last time I gave you a ring."

"Not a chance. You're stuck with me."

"I was hoping you would say that, because now we're going to be working together too."

"Are you kidding?"

"No, ma'am. I can't be married to the CFO of a construction company. I would say that's a huge conflict of interest."

"Are you sure? I know how much you love your job."

He kissed my hand. "I love you more. And your dad is making it worth my while. But enough talk about work. I have something for you and the baby." He handed me the second bag.

I couldn't take it right away. Another contraction hit. I took his hand back and squeezed.

"Breathe, Mel."

"I feel like I can't."

"You can. In through your nose and out through your mouth," he coached me over and over.

I made it through and released a large breath. "I can't imagine these getting worse."

"You can do this. Open the bag. Maybe it will take your mind off the pain for a minute."

I reached in the bag and pulled out a key attached to a red ribbon. "What's this?"

"The reason I haven't been as attentive as I've wanted to be."

I stared at the key. "I'm confused."

"I wanted to show you, but after I asked your dad this

morning for his blessing to marry you, I figured I better tell you sooner rather than later."

I felt so stupid now worrying about Declan's feelings, but could you blame me after everything I'd been through?

"Mel," he paused. "I bought the red bungalow."

"What?" I had a million questions, but couldn't focus on them right now.

"Yeah, and despite the high price, it needed some work. I wanted it to be perfect for you, for our baby."

My hand covered my heart. "Our baby."

"Our baby."

"I love you, Declan Shaw."

∾⎇⎇

I still couldn't believe he was here. I held the world in my hands, all eight pounds, four ounces of him, while resting in the arms of the man I loved, exhausted but elated. It was the middle of the night before I kissed the head of the most perfect baby. His soft dark hair was done up in a mohawk per the nurse who was in love with his full head of hair. He was only a few hours old, but it was like he had always existed. How did I ever live without him? Or the man who held me?

Declan kissed my head. "You were amazing."

"I didn't feel that way." Especially after hours of labor.

"Take it from me. I'm in awe of you and your body."

"Thank you for getting me through it. I couldn't have done it without you."

"I was just crowd control. You did all the heavy lifting."

He spoke of my crazy family and friends. Since Tamara decided she was coming to the hospital, Momma couldn't be outdone despite her major medical phobia. First sign of a needle and Momma went down. Daddy caught her, thank goodness. She still insisted on staying, which meant Daddy had to watch over her. Then the best friends thought they should be here too, which meant my doctor wasn't as focused as he needed to be. And since Halle's boyfriend, aka my doctor, was here, Heather called in her doctor.

And there I was feeling like my insides were being ripped apart every five minutes or so. Declan never left my side amidst the chaos, but he finally took control of the situation. "Everyone out," he shouted above the noise. He meant business and I never loved him more.

The experience became much more intimate after that, and what I always envisioned it would be. It was the hardest, but most wonderful experience.

"Can I hold him?" Declan, like me, couldn't get enough of him.

I kissed his soft cheek before placing him in Declan's eager arms. He barely stirred. He had hardly cried since he entered the world. He seemed content to be wrapped up and held. His momma liked that too.

Declan held him close, captivated by this little man who'd entered our lives. "I hope I can be the father he needs me to be."

"I'm not worried at all." I held Dixon Shaw's little hand. I had finally decided on a name. Daddy and Declan were both thrilled.

Declan kissed my head. "Mel, I wish my eighteen-year-old self could have pictured this. I would never have walked away. I shudder to think how I could have missed out on this, on you, on our son. I regret all the time we missed out on."

I thought for a moment as I gazed at the two most important people in my life. I thought about regret and our time apart. I thought about this moment. "I do too, but…I think it's made the here and now sweeter than it ever would have been."

Epilogue

Six Months Later

I woke up to an out of tune version of "California Dreaming" by the Mamas and Papas over the baby monitor. It was Dixon's favorite, as was the man that was singing to him off key. I stretched and smiled in our bed. I hadn't even heard Dixon fuss. I looked at the time, it was a little past 4:00 a.m. It had been a while since Dixon had woken up so early. He finally got his days and nights figured out a few months ago. Thank goodness. The whole lactating zombie prediction was real for several weeks. Declan was such a trooper. We didn't get to have the typical newlywed experience, but I wouldn't have traded these last six months for anything, even if I had never been more exhausted. Or changed my shirt more than I cared to remember.

I looked around at our bedroom, it spoke of Declan's love. The shiplap walls were already filled with photos of our small family. I swore Declan took several pictures of Dixon a day. I always seemed to end up in a few, and now some of those were displayed on our walls along with some professional shots.

I yawned and threw off our coral ruffled comforter. Declan was a good enough man to not care that our bed had a more feminine flair. I crept next door, tiptoeing on the ash wood flooring that had to be refinished before we could move in. I loved our red bungalow, but not as much as the scene in the dude ranch themed nursery that my best friends so skillfully decorated. My favorite thing about it was the barnyard doors with Dixon's name on them and the cowhide rug. And of course, the retro record player that had gotten plenty of use. Jimmy was happy to hear that Dixon was a huge Simon and Garfunkel fan.

I leaned against the door and watched my life, my husband and my son. Declan held our baby against his bare chest with such tenderness, singing and lulling him gently as he paced the floor with him. Dixon looked right at home snuggled against his daddy. I never knew such love existed until that little man came into my life. He seemed to change every day. His personality was taking shape. And though he looked like Greyson with his dark hair that had a little curl in it and a nose just like his, Dixon's happy demeanor was all Declan.

Dixon was full of smiles and giggles. And though he wasn't saying real words yet, he talked all the time. We'd had some of the best conversations. He was also mobile now, rolling every which way and any day now he was going to be crawling. He'd been rocking back and forth on his hands and knees threatening to the past few days. I wanted to hit the pause button, but I also wanted to see who he was going to become.

Declan caught me admiring him. He looked amazing even in the middle of the night with his bed head hair. He gave me a crooked grin. "Sorry, I woke you." He used hushed tones.

I met him in the middle of the room.

Declan took me in his arms too. There we swayed together with our love between us. I kissed Dixon's sweet head. I breathed in his baby scent. I could never get enough of him or the man that held us.

"I didn't even hear him wake. Is he okay?"

"His diaper was wet." That was the one thing Dixon fussed about.

"You should have woken me up. It was my turn to get up with him."

Declan kissed my forehead. "I don't mind at all and I know how rough these past couple of weeks have been for you." He spoke of Tamara.

She was fading fast. She had round the clock in-home hospice care now. My heart was aching at the thought of losing her. Though our relationship had never been the same since the divorce, I loved her and at times had felt the closeness we once had. And did she ever love Dixon. I had been spending as much time with her as I could, even though that meant being around my ex-husband, the bank president. He worked his magic as only he could to keep his job. It didn't surprise me. He usually got what he wanted. But being around him more than anything was taking its toll. He was still having a hard time letting go, which was odd considering last year at this time he couldn't seem to get rid of me fast enough. But it didn't matter.

This moment mattered with my husband and son. These were my people.

"Thank you for being so understanding."

"You don't have to thank me…unless." I could hear the smile in his voice. "We are both awake and our son is sound asleep. I could do with some alone time with my wife."

With a newborn, sometimes it felt like the stars had to align for that to happen, but we made sure to sneak in anytime we could. "I'll race you to our room." I kissed our baby one more time.

Declan gently laid down our slumbering angel in his crib, and before I could even take a step toward the door, I found myself swept off my feet. I ran my hand against his bare chest and reveled in being held close.

"One of these days I need to take you on a real honeymoon." He carried me to our room, kissing me between words.

I wasn't ready to leave our little man yet and honestly I don't think Declan was either.

My toes still curled and my heart pounded with each touch, just like when I was sixteen, except it had only gotten better with time. "I don't care where I am, as long as it's with you and Dixon."

He pulled me closer and buried his head in my neck. "Mrs. Shaw, I love it when you talk like that."

"I know something you love even more."

He groaned against my ear. "You are the best wife ever."

About the Author

JENNIFER PEEL IS THE AWARD-WINNING BESTSELLING author of the Dating by Design and Women of Merryton series, as well as several other contemporary romances. Though she lives and breathes writing, her first love is her family. She is the mother of three amazing kiddos and has recently added the title of mother-in-law, with the addition of two terrific sons-in-law. She's been married to her best friend and partner in crime for a lot longer than seems possible. Some of her favorite things are late night talks, beach vacations, the mountains, pink bubble gum ice cream, tours of model homes, and Southern living. She can frequently be found with her laptop on, fingers typing away, indulging in chocolate milk, and writing out the stories that are constantly swirling through her head. To learn more about Jennifer and her books, visit her website at www.jenniferpeel.com.

If you enjoyed this book, please rate and review it on
Amazon.com & Goodreads

You can also connect with her on
Facebook & Twitter (@jpeel_author)

Other books by Jennifer Peel:
Other Side of the Wall
The Girl in Seat 24B
Professional Boundaries
House Divided
Trouble in Loveland
How to Get Over Your Ex in Ninety Days
Paige's Turn
Hit and Run Love: A Magnolias and Moonshine Novella

The Women of Merryton Series:
Jessie Belle — Book One
Taylor Lynne — Book Two
Rachel Laine —Book Three

The Dating by Design Series:
His Personal Relationship Manager — Book One
Statistically Improbable — Book Two
Narcissistic Tendencies — Book Three (Coming Soon)

The Piano and Promises Series:
Christopher and Jaime—Book One
Beck and Call—Book Two
Cole and Jillian—Book Three

Made in the USA
Middletown, DE
04 March 2020